THE MO TOBE

BOOK 1

1900 - 1960

A Novel

by

Alana Beth Davies

Copyright © Alana Beth Davies
Edited and Published by © Awduresau Cymru Publishing (ACP)

First published in paperback in May 2024

Alana Beth Davies has asserted her right under the Copyright, Designs & Patents Act 1988, to be identified as the author of this work.

All rights reserved. No part of this publication may be reproduced, stored in a retrieval system, or transmitted, in any form or by any means without the prior written permission of the publisher, nor be otherwise circulated in any form of binding or cover other than in which it is published and without a similar condition being imposed on the subsequent purchaser.

This book is a work of fiction and, except in the case of historical fact, any resemblance to actual persons, living or dead, is purely coincidental. Every effort has been made to obtain the necessary permissions with reference to quotes. We apologize for any omissions in this respect and will be pleased to make the appropriate acknowledgements in any future edition.

Cover picture from an original watercolour
by Clive Drake (Bridgend)

Awduresau Cymru Publishing (ACP)
www.acpeditandpublish.com
Swansea

This book is dedicated to all mothers everywhere.

CONTENTS

CHAPTER	PLACES	YEAR/S	PAGE
One	Ireland	1916	7
Two	Ireland	1888	26
Three	Ireland	1916	35
Four	Wales	1916	42
Five	Wales	1940	53
Six	Wales	1916 - 1926	77
Seven	Wales	1942	94
Eight	Ireland	1942	98
Nine	Wales	1942	114
Ten	Ireland	1942	122
Eleven	Ireland	1942	134
Twelve	Wales	1953	144
Thirteen	Persia	1948	151
Fourteen	Wales	1950	158
Fifteen	Wales	1942-1948	167
Sixteen	Wales	1956	171
Seventeen	Wales	1957	177
Eighteen	Ireland	1959	195
Nineteen	Wales	1959	212
Twenty	Wales	1960	227
Twenty One	Wales	1960	240
Glossary			245
Also by …			247
Acknowledgements			249

THE MOTHERS OF TOBERGELL
CHAPTER ONE
IRELAND
1916

DUBLIN

It's chilly on the dockside. She pulls her knitted shawl tighter, stamps her feet, just a little. Just enough for warmth; not enough to cause a fuss, make a scene. Careful not to let her boots slip on the wet cobbles. She isn't looking at the water. One glance had been enough, seeing the choppy grey peaks, the foam spluttering up, making her want to heave. But she feels the spray, ever so light, ever so gentle, kissing her face, slowly soaking her flannel skirts. She doesn't look behind her either, doesn't move, but she knows what's left of the building there, its classical columns pitted with shot, spattered with blood. She can hear the sounds of gunfire, the screaming of loud commands – it's in her head. She wasn't there.

Men are moving, walking quickly, talking quickly in the Irish way, minds on their jobs. Rough men, but city men. Ropes pulled, cargoes heaved, banter and grunts exchanged, not slowing them down, adding a rhythm to their work. Women too, doing men's work, only distinguishable by their head coverings.

They wouldn't be here, surely! They wouldn't travel all this way! Even if they knew. Even if Ma had told them. But she wouldn't. Big strapping lads they were, full of laughter in the drink, scowling in the morning. And they would defend their little sister's honour with – if not their lives, then their fists. She smiles at the thought. Her honour indeed! She envied them sometimes, the boys, the men. Envied the camaraderie, the brotherly love, shown physically only through football. Or war.

And it's almost time now. She picks up the worn carpet bag from where it sits near her feet, as the boat is chugging up the Liffey, ready to take her away.

THE POST OFFICE

The clash and clang of ripped metal, the remorseless firing of cannons, the crunch of masonry as it crumbled beneath the barrage of shot – the noise alone was agonising. And then – the screams of men as they fell, limbs torn apart, heads with gaping wounds, as they swore, or cried for their mothers and Jesus. Bare-footed children crept under the eyes of the soldiers to raid anything they could from the shops. Dancing slippers and fur stoles, decanters and wooden platters, it was all fair game, all part of the fun, all treasures unseen before, to be enjoyed before shouts and rifles shooed them away again. Flames shot into the air as fires took hold around the rebels' headquarters.

Private Alfred John Hughes, seventeen, watched as men, or boys just like him, fell. And he could not move. Couldn't shoot, couldn't walk, couldn't run. But no-one seemed to notice. Cold sweat ran down his thin face, gathering in the scant forest of stubble. He stared around him, took a step backwards. Shot for cowardice, or bayoneted while doing his duty? That was his choice. His body trembled, tears joined the sweat in a shameful stream, as he prayed for salvation or rescue.

Trucks were moving behind the ranks of soldiers now, His Majesty's officers yelling to the troops, drivers shouting to the firing mob as the last of the rebels came out, hands and heads held high, waving a torn scarlet shirt that this morning had been white, signalling that, once again, they were on the losing side.

Prisoners were marched away from the smashed Palladian building by the constabulary; bodies were loaded roughly onto stretchers, the injured dragged to waiting trucks. Civilians too, in workaday clothes, carrying bags or baskets, were sprawled on the ground, killed or maimed as collateral damage. Two horses lay on the street where they'd been shot five days ago. The smell of burning wood and flesh, and the choking clouds of gun smoke filled the air and the nostrils, stung the eyes.

And still Fred didn't move.

A bullet spat into his leg and he looked down at it in surprise. No pain at first, just the knowledge that something wasn't right, that something had happened. He looked up, across O'Connell Street, to the low huddle of buildings that had once been shops and offices, from where the shot must have come, and he saw him. A boy like himself, dressed in the grey-green serge tunic and breeches of the Irish Volunteers.

The shooter stopped. Fred saw the boy's face, white with its own fear, flushed with an unhealthy glow, as he turned and ran.

Fred fell to the ground. His leg was bleeding, would no longer hold him, but he couldn't just stay here. Would the boy return? With his fellow rebels? Would they finish him off? There were rebel snipers on the roof too, some only children. Fred dragged himself to the side of the road. Rows of huge rubber tyres formed a barricade, gave him the cover he sought as he lurched back against a fence. Then, one by one, the engines growled into life, shambled forward in a battered green convoy, till just one was left. Silent and still. Was it an army truck? Just a van? Fred didn't care. He tried to climb into the empty rear of the vehicle, but all strength was gone, his arms as weak as saplings. Then hands, clammy and hot but welcome nevertheless, hands were pushing him, pulling him up, covering him with an old tarpaulin. He felt the engine growl under him, the sudden jerk as it moved forward, and the truck rumbled through the countryside. The bullet was working its way like a knife, damaging the tissue that lay in its path, until stopped by bone. If he could have seen it, Fred would have noticed the red puffy ring forming around the entry wound in his hot flesh, the blackening at the edges. But he couldn't see it. The fabric of a soldier's uniform is tough. Not quite tough enough to stop a bullet, but thick enough to cover its damage.

Fred gagged at the stench of rubber, fetid oil and animal faeces. And as he felt the vibrations beneath him, heard the noise of the engine, his world went black.

TOBERGELL

'They say it was terrible bad down there Eugene! Blood and guts and ...'

'We'll have none of that language thank you, Aidan! Now stop your blathering and help your brother clean the truck!'

'Okay so, Ma. I'll go and ...'

'Eugene – did you sell the lot?'

'Yes Ma, no trouble at all. They're terrible keen on our lambs!'

'Well, fighting or no fighting, they need to eat. They ...'

'Ma! Ma! Eugene! Holy mother of God!'

'Aidan! What the devil are you shouting about now? And you can stop that papist talk soon as you like!'

Blanche Cockin picked up her booted feet and strode across the yard, swept clean that very morning, and marched to the muddy gateway where her eldest son had drawn up the van, and where her youngest now stood, hollering. Under five feet tall and almost as wide, Blanche held herself like a six-footer. Her head was held erect, her salt-and-pepper hair pulled back in a severe bun, as her sapphire eyes squinted in the Easter sun. Her patched skirt and her husband's ticking shirt did nothing to take away her authority. And while Aidan clacked and babbled at her side before the open van doors, she said not a word.

A full minute passed.

'Get him out, you two.' Blanche's voice was calm. 'Get him out, and let's have a look at him.'

A boy. Sweating and shivering like the ague. Muttering and mumbling. He lay, curled like a baby, sticky on the matting of wheat bags and spilled animal feed, lying against the rubber sheeting at the back. Blood covered his hands.

'Take him to the barn. Put him on some clean straw.'

Eugene picked the lad up and laid him across his shoulders. It was easy. Hadn't he done it a hundred times with one brother or another, in jest or in drunkenness? A twisted leg never hindered him. So he carried the boy to the barn, laid him down on the straw as gently as he would a lamb.

* * *

'Sorry Ma, time ran away!'

Daisy panted, pulled off her shawl, grabbed her pinny.

'How many tonight?'

She caught back her long hair and twisted it into a copper knot, holding the grips between her teeth until they were needed. She held her hands under the trickle from the brass tap over the bosh.

'Rain trough's drying up again, Mammy!' she called.

'How many? How many d'you think, girl? Honest to God!'

Daisy took five heavy earthenware platters from the dresser shelf, piling them into the crook of her arm.

'I mean - the man? Is he not to have any supper?'

Blanche raised her head, quick as a pigeon.

'Your nose will get you in trouble one day, my girl!'

The plates laid out on the huge rough table, spaced just right, Daisy went to the dresser once more. She opened the right-hand drawer where the wearing cutlery was stored.

'But - is he not? Can I not take him a wee bite? Mebbe after supper?'

Blanche sighed.

'There'll be no coming with him, Daise. He hasn't long.'

The girl set about finishing the laying of the sturdy table, made as a wedding gift by her father, as if to demonstrate the large family he expected his wife to produce. And she hadn't disappointed.

Daisy loved this room, with its sweet smell of burning earth and baking bread, the warmth of the fire even in the coldest of winters, and the feel of the cool stone beneath her thin soles. Above the vast stone hearth the chimney breast was blackened by generations of fires. No longer any need for the spit now, nor the crane's arm fixed to hold the pots and the kettles. Blanche Cockin was the proud owner of an iron cooking range. No need to bend over the smoking peat-bog turf. But still the fire in the hearth burned, as the sides of bacon cured in the smoke that curled to meet them, hanging from the lethal-looking ceiling hooks.

The boys came in, boots heavy on the flagstones, voices raucous, patting her head or ruffling her hair, the little sister, the baby, the wee one. But the noise stopped as they sat, heads bowed, prayers muttered, before they stretched for the bread to dip, the beakers to drink. Rich food they may have had growing or grazing all around them, but that was for trading, for making a living, not for wasting at the table. So they tucked into the cabbage and potato stew as they fished around for the occasional morsel of mutton, careful of their manners under their mother's watchful eye.

'Is Da no in for supper, Ma?'

Daisy felt Aidan's boot against her shin. She shot him a scowl.

'He's busy with Mr McIver,' said Blanche, dishing out more stew whether they wanted it or not. Used to feeding six men, her cooking portions had stayed the same for three, so she eked out the meal with water and more tatties, as if the missing three were about to come stomping in to join their brothers. But tonight there were only two of her men. The women's helpings didn't count.

The meal was finished in silence, as the platters were emptied and refilled and emptied again. Blanche steered her eyes away from her husband's waiting plate, knowing he would want only bread and cheese. If he came home.

Daisy opened her mouth to speak, but her mother got there first.

'Yes! Go on then! For all the good it'll do him. And don't stop long!'

The girl didn't need to be told twice. She jumped to her feet, dipped a chunk of bread into the juice at the bottom of the pot, and carried it, one hand under the other to catch the drips, out through the back door.

The man – surely no more than a boy, surely no older than she was – lay where her brother had put him. His face was red, damp with sweat, droplets on his top lip where whiskers were starting to grow. His long tawny hair was matted. She could see blood on his hands, his clothes, but couldn't make out where it was coming from. Still, first things first.

'Can you hear me?' She knelt at the side of him.

'Can you open your eyes a wee bit? I've some food here for you.'

His eyes opened, slowly, as he tried to focus, the huge pupils gradually adjusting to the light of the lamp Daisy carried, the green-flecked grey becoming larger. His lips were dry, and he licked them with no spittle. The girl picked up the beaker, dipped the corner of her apron into the water, and touched his mouth with it. He gasped, then sucked greedily on the cloth.

'Don't rush it.'

She put the soaked bread to his mouth and he sucked that too, obediently slow. His eyes began to clear, and he stared at her. Daisy could feel the heat from his body, smell the sweat. She'd seen a fever before, and she knew what to do. She stripped him of most of his clothes; she lay wet straw on his temples and his wrists; she watched him shiver before she covered him loosely with a light sheet of canvas.

'I'll come back,' she said. 'I promise.'

Daisy kept her promise, permission grudgingly given by her mother, who popped in now and then throughout the night, making sure there was no malarky going on. Sick or no, you had to be careful. So the girl sat by the invalid, washed his hands, fed him trickles of water and sips of cold stew, while he sweated and panted and muttered, and by the morning his fever had broken. She wiped his forehead and tucked her apron around him.

'What's your name?'

Nothing.

'C'mon, you can tell me your name. I'm Daisy.' She smiled as she held his hand.

'Michael.' His voice was hoarse. 'Michael Byrne. Mick.'

'That's better. And where are you from?'

'Where's the other one?'

'What? What other one? There's only me. You must have been dreaming!' she laughed.

He raised himself up now, gripping her hand, frowning, urgent.

'The one in the van.'

This one was a soldier, that much was clear. Hidden from sight by the heavy tarpaulin and the empty sacks, he lay still as a corpse. His fair hair was cut to the scalp. There was nothing of him - light as a colt if it weren't for his uniform. Skinny or not, it took both brothers to carry him into the barn and lay him down on a bale opposite the first. Out cold, he was. And no wonder, with the blood matting the khaki wool from groin to ankle; a festering bullet wound, a livid hole in an unholy cushion of pus, with blood dried and clotted, all too clear when Eugene cut away the cloth. He hadn't a hope.

They left him as comfortable as they could, hung their heads, walked away, back to the kitchen and the fields and the cowsheds, back to their lives.

'Mr McIver!'

Daisy waited till her father had stumped away, angry as always, leaving the vet in the vegetable garden. She knew her father would never agree, would shout and rant and tell her to know her place. So she had waited.

'What is it, Daisy?' The vet, with the build of a stallion and the hands of a pianist, looked down at her, surprised and amused.

He listened to her. He didn't laugh, but he smiled.

'I'm a vetinarian, Daisy. Not a doctor. Not a surgeon. What you're asking is impossible.'

'He'll die anyway. He will, won't he? You could try, couldn't you? You'd do it if our horse was shot. Or the dog.'

'You know what the doctor said, Daisy.' He spoke gently. 'He was left there too long, lass.'

'I know you can do it. Those books you gave me ... please!'

The fact that he was quiet for a moment raised her hopes.

'I'd need my instruments. And I'd need help.'

'I can help you! I want to! I'm going to be a nurse one day! Or maybe a doctor!'

And now he laughed.

'You're a child, Daisy. You're sixteen. There are things you shouldn't see.'

'Mr McIver, I live on a farm. With animals and five brothers. A wee bodeen on a poor bleeding soldier won't be frightening me away, will it now?'

It wasn't something to be kept secret for long. When Ambrose appeared in the kitchen at last, he beat the wooden table till the plates rattled, he bellowed and he blasphemed, but Daisy stood her ground.

'So, what would you have us do then, Da?'

'Us?' her father roared. 'Us? That's the last time McIver sets foot on my land! The last time he puts ideas ... the last time ...'

'I asked him to do it!' She was shouting now too, loud enough to be heard. 'It was my idea and I asked him! So don't be so stupid as to send away the one person around here you seem to talk to!'

Too much, too much. And she knew it. His hand swung across her face and sent her to the stone floor. Her cheek was blazing, her lip bleeding, as she staggered to her feet. Ambrose stared in shock, horrified at his actions. Her mother pushed her way between them then, stood flat-footed, her head tilted back as she looked up at her husband. Her voice was so quiet that all around was hushed, to make out the words she spat.

'You're no man, Ambrose Cockin. You're no man to treat your own daughter in such a way. I never thought you'd turn into your mother, cruel soul that she was. You wonder why the army won't take you? Watching your sons march off, treating us all like the enemy? What have you become, man?'

CHAPTER TWO
IRELAND
1888

BALLYBAILE

Blanche Allen was just right for him. Everyone said so. And if not everyone thought she was the most beautiful woman in the world, Blanche knew that he did. He loved her dark brown hair that she wore twisted into a bun at the nape of her neck. He loved her soft sapphire eyes that twinkled with mischief when they were together. He didn't think she was too short, or lacked child-bearing hips. She promised him many sons. It wasn't one of the promises she made in the fine Irish Church of Ballybaile as her family looked on, nodding as if to say, 'That's another one off our hands!', but a vow sacred to her, even at eighteen.

Ambrose Cockin. Just three years older. Farmer. Well, son of a farmer, but he'd have his own place one day. And in the meantime, the young couple would live with his parents, have their own bedroom, and share everything else, including the work: he on the land, and she in the house. Their nights alone were what Blanche lived for. He was tender, loving, if vigorous in their bed. She would lay awake while he slept, drained by their lovemaking, and she would stroke his too-long hair, red as a shepherd's delight, silky as new milk. The days were to be endured, but that was no surprise. Ambrose's father was a man of few words, preferring the company of his livestock, although not unkind to Blanche. But his mother Agnes was a dour woman, jealous of her domain, jealous of her son and resentful of his little floozy. She spoke little, frowned much, the creases on her brow as settled as a ploughed field in a drought, and she shook her head, seemingly in disbelief or sorrow, at everything Blanche did. When the younger woman offered to make Ambrose's supper, her mother-in-law glowered.

'You'll do no such thing. That's a mother's duty.'

True to her promise, Blanche was pregnant within three months. Ambrose looked forward to the day his son would be born – of course, it had to be a son – and he left the rest to his young wife. What did he know about carrying and birthing? No, best left to the women. Agnes lost no opportunity to criticise Daisy, silently or otherwise, but Ambrose remained blissfully unaware. As her belly swelled, as her movements slowed, Blanche found herself apologising, tripping, making mistakes, as if confirming her mother-in-law's assumptions. Blanche didn't grumble. She endured it. She fetched and carried, swept and scrubbed, peeled and mashed, without a word of complaint. Never a word. Even when the pains started, not a word. But when the cushioning liquid trickled onto the floor, she knew it was close. So she told Agnes.

'Be about your business then,' was all her mother-in-law said.

'But – my ma? And ... and ... Ambrose?'

'This is no place for menfolk! Get to your bed. I'll get cloths and water. The rest is up to you.'

When Ambrose ambled into the house for his supper, there was no Blanche to greet him. His mother said nothing till he was sitting at her table, eating her food.

'Your wain is on the way. You'll hear it soon enough.'

Animal sounds escaping Blanche's dry mouth, she writhed in agony for hours before her mother Deirdre arrived. Ambrose ran the two miles to fetch her and a dogcart carried them back. Deidre hurried up the creaking stairs, ignoring Agnes. Her daughter lay in a pile of soiled and bloodied sheets, spasms seizing her body; a bloodless face, a rasping breath. A tiny leg, unmoving, blue, was visible between her thighs.

'Ambrose! The midwife! Be quick now!'

The child would be dead of course. Deirdre had to do what she could. She felt around the foot, around the leg, put her fingers inside to loosen the swollen flesh that held it. She pushed her fingers up, up, till she felt the tiny buttocks; found the matching leg, folded back. So near to birth, so close to life. Tears mingling with her daughter's blood, she pulled. She pulled the little mite until she thought it would snap, until Blanche's screams pierced her. And still she pulled. And there was this helpless bloody creature lying on the stained linen, its leg horribly twisted, yelling its little head off.

Eugene, they called him.

The fact that Blanche was able to give birth again, after the mauling her body had received, was remarkable, and in the years following, more sons came. Bertie, Charlie, Des, and little Aidan.

TOBERGELL

Blanche had kept her promise, and at last Ambrose kept his. They moved into their rented stone cottage with its apron of land in the hamlet of Tobergell, when Bertie was in nappies and Charlie still at the breast. Eugene, with the knotted shillelagh his father had cut to size for him, hobbled along, never complaining. Baby number four was on the way, and Blanche could not get away from Agnes quickly enough. She'd done her penance, over and above, and now she had her own kitchen, her own garden, and Ambrose had two acres to graze his solitary cow and his tiny flock of sheep, to grow his cereals and his vegetables. Bláth Cottage, they called it. They welcomed little Des into the world, and then, three years after Aidan's surprise arrival, a daughter. Margaret, known as Daisy.

Five sons. Strong healthy sons, even the one with a twisted leg. They would work the farm, Blanche thought. Build it up, help their Da. But she always knew the time would come when they would look ahead, look to their own futures. When they'd see that little acreage split into five. Six, while their Da was alive. And it wouldn't sustain them.

Des was the first to go. At sixteen, he found work with the big Belfast shipbuilders Harland and

Wolff, building the finest liner that ever floated. With every rivet he set, he knew what he wanted. He liked handing a pay-packet to his mother each week, the only son that did so. And he liked the jingle of coins in his pocket when he joined the lads in the pub at the end of Saturday's shift. But it was the dream he was helping to build. A rivet here, another there, holding the huge steel structure together. He watched it grow, deck on top of deck, greater than any building he'd seen, until it was ready to be launched, to be towed to the fitting-out berth where the engines and funnels and interior would be put in place: the mahogany furnishings, the Turkish baths, the grand staircase.

Des, now eighteen, watched as soap and tallow were spread on the slipway to allow the Titanic easy passage into the river Lagan. And he knew he would follow her.

Blanche had tried to keep him home, God knows. All that year, while he saved and dreamed, she begged him, but it was no use, and she knew it. So when the great ship, fresh from Southampton and

Cherbourg, set sail again from Queenstown in the south, Des was on board. Steerage, at seven pounds and fifteen shillings, one way. He would make his fortune in New York, he had told his mother.

He might have survived, Blanche insisted.

Two years later, she said goodbye to another two sons. Not for money or comradeship, although they would have both. Britain was at war, and Irishmen were being urged to join the fight, vanquish the foe, the commanders in London using every persuasive device to appeal to poetic souls. Bertie and Charlie signed up.

'We have to fight, Ma.' Bertie was gentle, kind, mindful of his mother's feeling, but resolved. 'We're British, aren't we? It's our duty.'

'Yeah, we're not like those traitorous scum in the south!' railed Charlie. 'Sorry, Ma, but so they are!'

And they went, full of the romance of a noble cause, and Blanche watched. Thank God Eugene had no hope of being accepted. Aidan champed at the bit to join his brothers, wear the uniform, but at sixteen he was too young. Small mercies. And the most bitter pill for Ambrose to swallow – at forty-seven he was too old.

And so Blanche made her stew for three men, not her half-dozen, and knew why Ambrose never joined them.

CHAPTER THREE
IRELAND
1916

TOBERGELL

Mick Byrne had watched as the soldier was carried in. He'd wanted to look away but could not. The limp body and the drenched khaki drew his eyes, in horror at what he had done, and hatred at what that uniform stood for. It had all seemed so clear, so right. When he and the other lads of Na Fíanna Éireann had listened to the words of Pádraig Pearse, he saw that gentle Gaelic scholar transformed into an angry man, outraged by injustice. And Mick had taken on his mantle, worn it with pride, the vision pure and true. But now, the reality was sordid and messy. This wasn't the glorious reckoning he'd marched for.

So he crept to the furthest corner of the barn, and he watched, his speckled eyes darting to the door, his untried muscles tensing each time someone entered. Mick ate the broth, drank the water that was brought him, and he said nothing. Daisy comforted the boy as best she could; she held him, she lay down with him, maybe for a bit longer than her mother would have approved. She was kind to the poor lad. But her efforts were concentrated on tending to Fred.

Mick knew he must go. Soon, before the other boy recognised him. He planned his exit well. He waited till night time, pulled on the jacket he'd seen hanging on a nail, been eyeing for days, and stuffed his supper bread into a pocket. He walked on the soft straw to the door, stopped and looked down at his fellow traveller, sick because of him, hurt because of him. Maybe dying because of him. Just another boy, like him, like his Fianna compatriots on the Dublin streets, all with mothers at home, waiting. But this one was here, safe and cared for, because of him too.

The bullet was out but still Fred lay, fever-ridden now, sweating and shivering, his face an unhealthy rosy glow. Daisy had found his papers, knew his name, his age, where he was from, and she knew he was a soldier, but there were questions she wanted to ask. Why was he over here when he should have been in France, or Persia? Da didn't speak of the war, but Ma couldn't help but follow every report, thinking of her two sons. Daisy knew the British army was desperate. Eugene had driven the van all the way back from Dublin; she knew there was fighting down there, but surely the army would prevail over a rabble of rebels? So every day she bathed Fred, and wiped him, dripped liquid into his mouth, and waited for him to recover.

When he mumbled and clung to her, when he blinked his half-open azure eyes at her, she smiled. When his temperature raged, she stripped him. When he shivered and tried to pull the sacking up over his chest, she climbed up next to him, held him, warmed him, soothed him. And as he recovered, she continued to lay with him. He talked to her, about his home and his brothers and the hills that took all the breath out of them, about the bay and the ships and the pier and the Mumbles railway.

'But I wanted to see more,' he told her, still feverish, anguished. 'I didn't ... I never ...'

When he wept, she kissed him; and when she felt his hardness, she knew what to do. She helped him, and it was the most natural thing in the world.

* * *

'I'm carrying, Ma.'

How else was she to say it?

Blanche sat heavily on the kitchen chair, put her head in her hands.

Daisy had expected the fury and the fire, not the fear and the tears she saw. Her mother wept quietly, then stopped abruptly, wiped her eyes with her apron, and stood, upright again.

'You cannot tell your Da. You cannot. He'd kill the boy. Nobody to put a ring on your finger then! And you, sent to the Sisters of Mercy? No, you cannot tell your Da.'

Blanche was pacing now, rubbing her hands down her apron, muttering her thoughts as they simmered and bubbled.

'He's on the mend then, the boy. So – you'll go away, get married, not a word. Your cousin in Fermanagh, she'll take you, you can marry there. Then ...'

'Ma, we can't.'

Blanche looked blank.

'He's going back, Ma. He's going back home. To Wales. To the army, I suppose.'

Silence. Then,

'Fine lad you've got there, Margaret!'

There was the fire, the fury.

'Leave you to the shame, would he? Well, mebbe we should tell your Da! Mebbe he'll get his shotgun out! Mebbe ...'

'Mammy! Stop! He wants me to go with him! To marry him! He ... he loves me, Ma.'

DUBLIN

Daisy pulled her shawl across her, stamped her feet for warmth again on the cool September morning. She had waved her mother off in the dim light of daybreak, watched the van as it lurched away.

'You'll be over the water before they know you've gone. They won't argue with me. If they knew ... dear Lord, if they knew! And your Da ... I'll handle him. I'll be saying no word of the babby though.'

The early morning drive had been a long one, a noisy one too, with crunching gears and whining engine as Blanche bumped along, unused to handling the vehicle since Eugene had taken over. Daisy turned in the passenger seat to watch the scene race by. She'd never been further than the village before, and here she was, going miles. The road wound its way through the countryside, past fields and farms, grass and gorse, then rows of cottages, villages, towns. The houses grew bigger, the roads wider;

cars, lorries, carts and carriages, and bicycles, so many bicycles.

As they stood on the dockside, Blanche at last pulled the girl to her.

'My wee girl,' she whispered. 'You'll be the mother now. God speed.' And she was gone.

CHAPTER FOUR
WALES
1916

SWANSEA

This homecoming was no celebration. Mary Ann wept when she saw her eldest son, the soldier, the fighter, as he stood at the door, looking this way, that way, wary, picking at a thread in his ill-fitting army-issue civilian suit. She looked at his brother George, and she was torn between relief at Bill's return and resentment that he should be the one to suffer. And what of Fred? It had been so long since she'd seen her youngest. Where was he now?

George was safe. He'd never had to enlist, never minded being classified as medically unfit. What's a burst eardrum compared with the shelling and the dirt and the water that Bill had lived through? Mary Ann saw George now, with his dark good looks, his disarming smile, his cocky air, a charmer with the ladies. For a moment, her love for each split her in two.

Bill was not the man who'd gone off to fight for his country two years ago, waving to her and his brothers, marching with his fellow volunteers, tall and handsome as any of them. The sights he'd seen, limbs torn from comrades as he watched, secretly praying it wouldn't be him next and suffering the guilt, all lived behind his shifting eyes. Now, he was a shadow. A ghost. No wounds to be seen, but scarred.

Mary Anne sat on the upright wooden chair next to the sink as she read the letter once more. She drew a breath.

'He's been hurt but he's coming home. I'll box his ears mind, running off to fight like that! Just a boy!' She dabbed her eyes as she read the letter again. 'Home for a bit at least.'

A proper homecoming this time, so soon after the last. Fred stood at the door, kit bag strap across his body, puttees spiralling neatly from ankle to knee. Surely he'd grown six inches since he left! Mary Ann silently thanked God for his grin and his wholesomeness, as she pulled him inside.

'Bill! Bill! Look who it is! It's our Freddie, come home to us!'

The cautious sideways glance was not what Fred had expected. Nor the emaciated figure, a parody of the big brother he remembered. Fred glanced at his mother, and she gave the slightest shake of her head.

'Bill! It's good to see you boyo! I bet you've got some stories ...'

Fred stopped. His mother shook her head again.

'Well, I've got some stories – and some news!'

He stood in the centre of the back-kitchen, bracing himself.

'I'm getting married!'

When Fred told his mother that Daisy had saved his life, had nursed him and wouldn't give up on him,

Mary Ann thawed a little. But inside she grieved for the boy he was. Getting married? At his age?

Fred omitted some details of course. One step at a time.

He knew her immediately. Wilted and pale, she stumbled off the Heather Rose as it pitched and dipped on its mooring. Khaki-clad lads swarmed past her, eager to greet families and bid their mates farewell, glad to be on home turf no matter how briefly, grateful for the brief respite the unscheduled stop allowed them, and anxious to reach shore before the ship sailed on to Bristol.

'Miss Daisy Cockin?' George was nothing if not polite.

Her face, already drawn and sickly, showed her disappointment. More than that. Confusion. Fear maybe.

'Freddie asked me to meet you. He couldn't get leave.' George was taking her bag as he spoke, gentle with her, leading her carefully towards a motor car.

God, there's nothing of her! he thought. But – well here's a turn up ...

'I'm George, by the way.' He helped her into the passenger seat, tucked the blanket over her knees. 'Fred's brother. Your brother too, pretty soon!' He smiled his charming smile.

George kept up his chatter as he drove out of the dockyards towards the city. He nodded towards the small mound under her shawl.

'Fred knows about it, then?'

'Of course he does!' She found her voice, thin and dry, but indignant.

George chuckled.

'Sorry love. Of course he does. And my Mam?'

Daisy's face flushed. Had he told his mother? What would they be expecting?

'So, never been to Swansea?' George recognised the confusion and continued his easy chat as the car purred on. 'It's a friendly enough place. Getting bigger all the time, thanks to copper. Coppertown we're called these days!' He laughed. 'Mam's pretty strict, but she's soft as butter underneath. Just got to know how to handle her. And Bill – well, Bill's had it rough. Fought in the Somme. He's not the same, poor bugger. Fred'll be home later.'

The Humber shuddered to a stop outside a short row of brick-built terraced houses. The ground around was rough, as if waiting for a continuation of homes at either end. George hopped out and ran to open the passenger door. He helped Daisy down, bowed with a flourish, and said, 'Welcome to Crispin Row!'

Daisy stepped carefully over the kerb. She followed George as he flung open the front door, and shouted, 'Mam! Mam! We're here!'

No sign of the Mam. Or of Fred. Only Bill's shuffling footsteps.

'Bill, my boy!' George put his arm around his brother's slender shoulders.

'Come and meet Freddie's girl! Daisy, she's called, remember? Lovely, isn't she?'

Bill gave a nod, turned, shuffled away again.

Even in the dim light, Daisy knew this house was larger than the cottage she was used to; stairs to the right, leading up to darkness, and a closed door to the left. Daisy put her hand out, touched the wooden dado rail that ran the length of the hall, separating the embossed, wood-stained paper below from the floral one above. She was glad of it. Her legs would not hold her much longer. The effects of the sea voyage, the nausea, the retching were still with her.

George led her into a kitchen, quite unlike her Ma's at home. A high wooden fireplace, surrounding a black polished range, dominated the room. A fire burned in a central grate – though not turf by the smell. Not wood either. What looked like oven doors either side, a hotplate above them, and above that a brass pole spanned the whole contraption. On the high mantelpiece a Napoleon Hat clock, flanked by a pair of ceramic spaniels, ticked, loud in the quiet room.

Daisy sat, uninvited, on the wooden settle that faced the fire. George brought her a glass of water.

'You look a bit peaky, love,' he said.

And Mary Ann walked in.

Just a matter of weeks, and it was all settled. Mary Ann had absorbed some shocks in her time - the early death of her husband, becoming the breadwinner of her family, one of her sons returned from war only half the man he was - and she absorbed this. Set against what might have happened to her youngest, the fact that he'd brought home a slip of a girl he'd got in trouble was as nothing. The wedding was arranged, quickly, while Daisy's condition could still be covered up with a few layers of strategically placed clothing. In place of a birth certificate, Daisy produced a letter signed by both her parents, swearing she was sixteen, giving permission for her to marry Alfred Hughes. Sixteen was a respectable age to marry. Yes, it was lawful for a girl to marry much younger, but sixteen was respectable, and that was important. Mary Ann looked at it. She could see that the two signatures were identical. She couldn't read it, but she looked at it. She shrugged.

So the young couple made their vows in Gendros English Congregational Church, a handful of curious neighbours in attendance. It was done. No fuss, no celebration, no fancy clothes. Home, then, to Crispin Row, to the whistling kettle on the hob and the waft of steaming cawl in the pot, to the new ways a young bride must learn. A young bride in someone else's house.

Mary Ann was kind, but blunt.

'I'm the mother in this household, bach. Remember that and we'll get on alright.'

The house itself was a fine one. The parlour, behind the closed door Daisy had passed, was used only to entertain the minister or other locally eminent visitors, standing ready to hold a wake when needed. The room smelled of lavender polish and camphor, and here was the best furniture: beautiful dining chairs with backs shaped into ovals, and tapestry on the seats; a glass-fronted china cabinet housing a complete set of what Daisy discovered was Swansea china; and in pride of place, a gramophone.

Three bedrooms each contained an enormous metal framed double bed, with quilted coverlets of varying quality, each high enough to need a step. Each room boasted a cabinet or dressing table with a jug and ewer, and a chamber pot, discreetly placed under the bed.

The yard was accessed through what the family called the back kitchen, itself a large and homely room full of comforting smells of mutton and cabbage, and housing a monster of a mangle. A long tin bath hung on the back door. Outside, a tiny square of concrete topped a steep flight of steps, leading down to an open area fringed by narrow borders of hardy violas and pansies. The space was dominated by a small wooden building that housed the lavatory. Inside, a wooden bench, scrubbed white and spotless, covered the metal pail just visible through the large hole cut in the wood. Neat squares cut from newspapers hung on a large iron nail, hammered into the back of the door, while the smell of creosote and Jeyes fluid masked some of the inevitable odour issuing constantly from the collected waste. A gate at the end of the yard led into a back lane, then, further down, into a garden, where vegetables grew alongside flowers and weeds.

It was a very fine house.

CHAPTER FIVE
WALES
1940

SWANSEA

Heads turned as he walked in. Was there a gasp? Certainly some whispers, some nudges. Nothing special to look at, unremarkable, except for what he wore. A charcoal grey suit, pin-striped, double breasted, proper turn-ups. Caitlin watched him in the huge cafeteria mirror as she sat at the counter with her cup of tea. Not many men in civvies these days. So what was he? Injured? A conchie? A spy? She smiled at the thought.

He was walking towards her.

He sat on the high stool next to hers. And he smiled too.

'I couldn't help looking at your hair,' he said to her. 'Can I buy you another drink? Name's Evan, by the way.'

* * *

'He's just a man, Mam! A man I met in Woolies caff!'

'Well, that says it all!' Daisy tidied perfectly tidy cushions and banged the kettle on the hob. 'That's not the way you've been brought up, my girl!'

Bill sat in the corner at the side of the hearth, head down, staring into the flames, as much a part of the furniture as any table or chair. Caitlin stood on tiptoe, admiring herself in the glass over the mantlepiece.

'You know nothing about him! Where's he from? Why isn't he in the army? Or the navy? What's he doing ...'

'Alright!' Caitlin sighed as she turned to face her mother. 'He's not in the army because he works in a restricted occupation. Yes, that's what it's called. He told me. I don't know what he does, but I think it's something to do with making bombs. He lives in Caereithin, with his mother and father. He's quite good looking, Rosemary thinks anyway.'

'Rosemary? So that's who you were with! A bit flighty, that one!'

'He looks a bit foreign, Chinese perhaps,' Caitlin went on.

'Caitlin!'

'But he's not!' she laughed. 'I asked him! No, he's got those – you know – high cheekbones. Just a bit.' And Caitlin danced around her mother, teasing her, daring her to be shocked.

Daisy smiled despite herself. Such a girl! Nothing she said swayed Caitlin, who, at twenty-three, was well able to choose her own friends. And her boyfriends. She'd lived in London on her own, for heaven's sake! Well, in the nurses' home, but same thing. She had looked forward to becoming a proper nurse, a qualified one – but all that ended with the war.

She'd argued with her mother, said they would need her in the hospital, said they couldn't do without her, but once the bombing started, once she saw bodies being carried out of buildings whose walls were blasted off; once she'd seen inside bedrooms, wallpaper intact, open to the elements, grotesque half-built structures where people had once lived, her pleading was half-hearted. She was grateful to her mother for insisting she return home, although she would not admit it. Almost November now, and the nightly bombing still went on in the capital. Caitlin thought of the people going about their lives as she had, routinely walking into underground tunnels at the sound of sirens, taking it in their stride. Except they didn't. These were people with families, jobs, loves and heartaches. And she wouldn't be one of them any more.

Daisy was only too glad to give her daughter the excuse she needed to come home. She thought of her brother Charlie, dead on the Somme at twenty-four, though his mother hadn't known it ... and Bertie, who might as well have been. That had been called the war to end all wars. Except it wasn't.

'So where's Meg tonight, Mam?' Caitlin pursed her lips, closing them over a fold in her handkerchief. She wouldn't smudge anyone's shirt now. She admired the crimson kiss on the white starched linen, before she turned to check that her stocking seams were straight.

'My last pair,' she said, more to herself than her mother. 'It'll be gravy browning and eyebrow pencil next – unless I find a handsome American!' She laughed.

'Margaret's out.' Daisy expressed her disapproval in those two words.

'Come on Mam! Nothing wrong with that!' Caitlin said, pulling on her jacket.

'Much too old for her. Best part of ten years.'

'I won't be late – say 'bye to Pops when he comes reeling in from the Marquis Arms!' Caitlin laughed as she stooped to kiss her mother on the cheek. 'Bye, Uncle Bill. And don't worry about Meg,' she added to her mother. 'She'll be grand.'

But worry Daisy did, of course. Each time her daughters left the house, each time Fred went to work on the buses, she worried. All the mothers did. Only the children weren't frightened by the bombs - all their games were war games, as they collected souvenirs from the shrapnel. After all, they were the good guys weren't they? Magazines were full of articles and cartoons saying so.

An anti-aircraft station sat above Penfilia now, by the racecourse, she'd heard. Round brick-built emergency water stations were all over Swansea. There was one on St Johns Road, another on Brondeg. People were cutting and cleaning oil drums to store water outside their houses, just in case. There was an ARP station by the Railmen's' Institute, and a first aid post was altering masks ready for the new gas. Good guys? It didn't matter. The bombing was indiscriminate. This was no game.

Margaret was the quiet one. The sensible one. Named for her mother, maybe the favourite one too. Well, in Caitlin's wake – bawling Caitlin, lively Caitlin – Margaret was a blessed relief. It was Bill who had started calling her Meg. Daisy hadn't argued, just pleased to see him showing some sign of life.

Meg knew he would leave her. She knew he must return to the fight once his arm was mended. Soon, all too soon. He would come back, but she was under no illusions about having any future with him. Graham Thomas was well and truly married. He would come home alright, but not to her. She never pressed him. She simply loved him. Her love was all-embracing, all-consuming, a fever of despair when he wasn't with her and passion when he was. Nothing and nobody else mattered; he was the only thing she cared about, more than she cared about herself.

'I've got a surprise for you, sweetheart!' he said now.

She looked up at him, smiled. Hugged his arm a little closer as they walked, making the most of the seclusion the hedges and trees in Brynmill Park offered.

'Don't you want to know?'

'Oh, yes, of course I do!'

'I've found us somewhere. A place for us.'

She didn't dare look at him.

'For us?' she said quietly. 'To live?'

'Well ... for us to meet. Perhaps you could live there though, Meg!'

She would not show him that tiny flicker of hope, or her disappointment when it was nipped out.

'That's wonderful, Gray!' she said. 'Where? Can I see it?'

He pulled her close. He stroked her hair, as the afternoon sun glinting through the branches made it glow gold and copper. He kissed the tip of her nose and she closed her eyes. He touched her lips with his. She felt herself quiver, heard herself give the familiar, involuntary gasp, before he dropped his arms.

'Not here, love. Not here.'

They walked on, out into the sunshine, past the ducks on the pond and the children feeding them.

The town was still reeling from the three days of sustained bombing that had turned houses and thoroughfares to rubble. Stretchers covered in blood sat outside an ARP hut and were being hosed down. People had slept under their stairs or in Anderson shelters, waking to see men digging in the wreckage, carrying out bodies, some alive. Many of the Swansea landmarks had disappeared. But Dogs Lane had survived.

The walk there was a long one, and it was rough cobbles when they got closer. This was a part of the town Meg didn't know. It had what her mother called 'a reputation', but she saw no ladies of the night leaning on gateposts or calling from upper floors. In fact, there were no gateposts. Narrow lanes barely separated rows of back-to-back terraces, front doors opening onto gravel and dirt. Washing lines hung between houses, limp laundry forming a series of sabre arches, mocking their union. The odour from the sewerage pipes, their contents not quite reaching the outfall into the bay, was everywhere. Children, some small, all grubby, peeped from behind bins or stared brazenly from the gutters, as the couple walked, Graham with his head down, Meg sometimes tripping, holding tight to his arm. From a pub at the end of the lane they could hear bawling music, mournful longings for an old Ireland the crooners had never seen.

'Here Meg, it's up here,' Graham said.

They turned right into an opening, a tarnished metal Jacob's ladder forming a zigzag up the wall of the building to their left. This, she supposed, would lead to their heaven.

* * *

Fred took her shoulders and held her away from him.

'Well, don't you look a picture!'

Caitlin's smile lit up her pretty face.

'Thank you Pops!' she said. 'Come on, not far to walk. Think you can make it?'

The little street gave a good showing, with neighbours from end to end turning out to wish her well. Children waved and cheered as she walked, arm in arm with her father, down to the church and through the lych gate. Her borrowed fur wrap and the refurbished straw hat cocked a snook at clothes rationing. She felt a million dollars. Evan was waiting, strictly formal, his fair hair Brylcreemed and slicked back, and she knew she was doing the right thing.

Their courtship had been a swift and quirky one. Following their first date, she hadn't expected to see him again. Hadn't really wanted to. Soldiers were in town, with their swagger and their loudness, their generosity and fun. But Evan had persisted. He wrote her letters – short ones, just keeping in touch, he said; not declaring undying love, nothing romantic. Nothing to make a girl swoon. He popped into the jewellers where she worked, smiled, asked her how she was. Never pestering for a second date, never staying too long. Once, he called at the house. Caitlin wasn't in, and her mother took pity on him as he stood at the door, rain dripping from the brim of his trilby. Daisy asked him in, made him a cup of tea, chatted for a while – then he was gone.

Within a fortnight, his doggedness had paid off; her curiosity had been piqued, and Caitlin agreed to meet him.

'He's a funny one, Meg!' she'd confided to her sister, who sat watching Caitlin prepare herself for the date. 'He's so serious! But he's clever, and he's very nice to me. And quite handsome in his way. Smart too. Wears lovely clothes ...' She dabbed powder onto her cheeks as she peered into her dressing table mirror. 'Too much rouge, d'you think?' she said.

'But do you like him, Caitlin? Really like him, I mean? Does he make your heart beat fast?'

'Come on Meg! You've been watching too many romance films! I'm no Vivien Leigh, and he certainly isn't Clark Gable!' Caitlin laughed, but she could see Meg thought differently. She put down the puff and turned in her seat.

'Oh no, not that Graham fellow? What would Mam think of if she knew you were carrying on with a married man? She only knows he's years older than you, and that's bad enough in her eyes!'

'She doesn't know him, Caitlin. None of you do. He's ... he's lovely. He's romantic and funny. He makes me laugh. He makes me feel ... I don't know. Like nothing else matters. Like – I don't care about anything else.' Meg looked up. 'I love him.'

The Carlton cinema was showing The Four Feathers, and although Caitlin may have preferred to see a comedy, or one of the romances she spoke so disparagingly about, she couldn't help but be impressed by the grandeur of the building, from its bowed front window to the richly panelled ceiling, polished marble columns, and elaborate spiral staircase.

More dates followed.

Evan treated her like a queen. He took her to dinner in the best restaurants in town; he sent flowers to her home, and chocolates to her work. He had a car - a Ford Prefect - and he drove them to idyllic places where he laid out picnics of pop and jam sandwiches. She'd been used to a rough-and-tumble kind of dating, with laughter and teasing and some kissing on the way home. This was different. She responded to his sincere compliments and his quiet solicitude with appreciation. His gentle humour, often hidden beneath his serious demeanour, was a new and subtle kind, and she liked it. But did he make her heart beat fast? Did she tingle with anticipation at the thought of him? She wanted to think so.

Caitlin would catch him looking at her, admiring her, and she would laugh, saying, 'It's just my hair you love, isn't it? Not me!'

And he would stroke the thick auburn waves, and smile, and tell her she was right, and she knew he loved her.

He took her to country places, talked to her about the land and the mountains and the rocks, the sea and the rivers. One day as they sat by a little stream – a pistle, he called it – he took her hand.

'Wnei di fy mhriodi i?' he asked.

She said yes. Afterwards, she would pretend she hadn't understood what she was agreeing to, hadn't know this was a proposal of marriage, but of course she had. After all, she wasn't getting any younger. It was time she settled down.

He took her, at last, to meet his parents. They walked up the hill to Caereithin, and Evan was quieter than usual. As they stood before the front gate, he said, 'You may think they're a bit different. From me, I mean. And from you. They ...'

Caitlin held his hand. She felt a tenderness towards him that was new to her.

'I just hope they like me!' she said.

A ticking of clocks greeted them as Evan opened the door. Dozens of clocks, it seemed. The shadowy hallway was lined with them, of various shapes and sizes, although the sounds seemed to come from all parts of the house.

'Oh, so this is the girl, is it?' his father said abruptly, as Evan drew his fiancée into the dark, stone-flagged living room. The old man wore his vest over his large belly, trouser braces hanging down at his sides. He remained seated in the armchair at the side of the open fireplace, twirling papers, stacking them into a wooden pot on the hearth.

'Hello, Mr Howells.'

'Spills,' he said, not looking up.

'And this is my mother,' Evan said, seeming to hold his breath, as indeed he had ever since entering the house. A short, stout woman walked in from what seemed to be the scullery, carefully carrying a cup and saucer, her hands shaking ever so slightly. Her body was enveloped in a floral wrap-around apron, her grey hair scraped back from her face and pulled into a bun, low on her neck. She said something that Caitlin didn't understand.

'Siarad Saesneg, Mam!'

'Sori, Bach!' She was hesitant. 'Nice to – to see you, cariad.'

She walked to stand in front of her husband and poured some of the tea from the cup unto the saucer. She tried to hand it to him.'

'Boeth, Merch! Boeth!' he shouted at her, and she pursed her lips and blew, very gently, onto the slopping liquid, before offering it to him again.

Caitlin and Evan didn't speak of their visit.

Caitlin took her time as she walked down the aisle on her father's arm. She savoured every moment. The pews were filled with friends and family, both sets of parents having turned out in best bib and tuckers. The scent of fresh flowers was everywhere, not quite extinguishing the smell of camphor and old wood that gave the building its familiar Sunday-school character. The organ played the bridal march as she made her way to the alter, and she beamed at her mother and sister as she passed.

Meg had shaken her head when her sister had asked her to be her bridesmaid. It would mean they'd have to get a special dress for her, she'd said. Had

Caitlin shown her disappointment? Perhaps. But old school friend Rosemary stepped up, and played the part well, whatever Daisy thought of her. She waltzed down the aisle after her friend now, elegant in her pink satin frock, and Meg smiled faintly in her direction, pleased that Caitlin had such a friend, pleased that she, Meg, didn't have to go through the ordeal. Graham wasn't there.

It was in this church that Daisy had married, twenty-four years earlier. She watched her eldest daughter with pride now, and some relief. Relief that Caitlin was not in the family way; relief that the new husband was able to give his bride a home of their own - as soon as it was ready anyway, even if it were just a couple of rooms above a baker's shop in Oxford Street. Daisy glanced at Meg – too thin, too pale, too sad – and her happiness faded a little. Where had her bright little girl gone? Always quiet, yes, but not like this, locked in her own world, paying lip service to everything around her, while a feverish melancholy seemed to grip her. What could a mother do? Daisy knew about the man, although she pretended not to. Better that way. So Daisy lifted her eyes instead to her elder daughter as she stood with her beau, giving their responses to the vicar's words.

The congregation burst into Love Divine. The couple shared a decorous and self-conscious kiss, then turned and walked back up the aisle. Guests turned as they walked past, smiled, nodded. The new Mr and Mrs Howells emerged, surrounded by laughter and confetti, and waved to the well-wishers. It will all blow over, Daisy thought to herself as she glanced once more at Meg. Least said, soonest mended.

Meg heard the news from the men in the pub where she pulled pints. She gripped the edge of the bar, watched her knuckles grow white, felt a pounding in her ears that had nothing to do with the loud and raucous exchanges in the tap room. No-one noticed. She pulled another pint.

It would be Graham's wife who'd had the telegram of course, who received the tea and sympathy, was allowed to weep, with neighbours rallying round, bringing hot dinners and faces set in mourning, dusting and fussing, wanting to hear any gory details and too polite to ask. Killed in action, was it? Shot? Gassed? Or was it the dysentery that got him? 'Here's a nice Victoria sponge, love. No children eh? Well that's a blessing ...'.

Not for Meg. She had no claim over him, no rights to tears and grief. She was as nothing. As the numbness wore off and the pain replaced it, she wanted to scream, to tear at her hair, her clothes. She did none of these. She lay face-down on the meagre mattress of her bed – their bed – and sobbed, pummelling the pillow until her strength was gone. Then she looked around the room, and its very bareness was a reminder of the total obsession that had been theirs. They had seen nothing, needed nothing, but each other. They had breathed as one, their hearts beat as one. Their minds totally in tune.

Hadn't he told her so? Hadn't he loved her beyond life? What did his wife know of that? Now she saw the hovel she lived in for what it was – no longer lit by her lover's presence, or his promise of return. The ambrosia tasted bitter in her mouth.

So she went home.

Did she want the good news or the bad news? Meg gave her mother a choice of sorts. Except there was no good news. A baby on the way - that should have been good news. But a bastard.

They sat at the kitchen table, facing each other, and the room was silent. Daisy had listened as Meg whispered the scandalous news. Could she talk of the love and passion she and Graham had for each other, of their plans, his promises? No, not to her mother. So she sat, her voice, quiet at the start, fading to a whisper before it died under her mother's hard stare.

It was Caitlin who broke the silence, running in, whipping off her scarf and shaking out her rain-soaked hair.

'I still have my key, Mam!' she laughed. Then, 'Meg! Haven't seen you in ages! Evan's just coming ...'

'Not now, Caitlin.'

'But ...'

'I said – not now!' Daisy shouted. Then, 'Sit down. Did you know about this? Has she told you? Do you know what your sister's become?'

'Mam, please!' Meg begged, tearful.

'Will someone please tell me what's going on?' Caitlin demanded. Then, 'Evan!' she shouted down the hall to her husband, 'I'll see you at home, okay?'

She sat.

'Well?'

'Go on then. Tell her.'

Meg looked up.

'Caitlin, I ...'

'Don't dilly-dally. Tell her.'

'I'm having ... Graham's baby. And he's dead. And ...' Meg's sobs overtook her. 'And I want to come home!'

Caitlin grabbed her sister's hand, held it, squeezed it.

'Oh love! Well of course you do! Of course! It'll be ...'

'No!'

Daisy's voice was low, firm.

'I'm sorry, Margaret. But - no. You can't live here. There's Uncle Bill, and Pops. And Caitlin and Evan, till their place is ready ... but we'll help with the rent on your place. You won't have to go on the parish.'

Daisy stood then, turned her back on the two girls, poked the cinders in the fireplace, steadied herself on the black surround.

'Mam! How could you?' Caitlin was in tears.

'Houl yer whisht girl!' her mother snapped.

Daisy couldn't explain it if she tried. But she saw herself, sixteen, pregnant, standing before a woman she didn't know, waiting for a man she barely knew. In this kitchen, a lifetime ago.

CHAPTER SIX
WALES
1916

SWANSEA

'So, you're Daisy, are you?' Mary Ann looked her up and down, her steel-grey eyes hard.

Daisy nodded, swallowed the bile that was rising in her throat again, pulled her shawl tighter, a vain attempt to cover the obvious.

'Fred didn't say. Didn't say a word about ... this. To his own mother!' Mary Ann looked into the girl's chalk white face, eyes huge. 'Well, what's done is done. We'll sort it.'

Daisy watched Fred stand, unsure, boyish, in front of his mother, waiting for the tongue-lashing, and, timid though she felt, Daisy went and stood beside him. It was months since she'd seen him; had only known him for a few weeks. Their liaison, so innocent at first, so naïve, had wakened the woman in her, but was now so far removed that it seemed another world. And here she was, the reality, waking from that dream, to stand by the stranger who would soon be her husband.

Mary Ann wasn't unkind, but it was clear who ruled the roost. Daisy learnt the ways of a respectable young wife reliant on the good nature of her mother-in-law. She cooked and she washed clothes, she turned the reluctant giant mangle till her hands were raw; she cleaned and she polished, much as she had done at home. She tried not to think of the farm, or of her mother, or her sullen Da. Her chest tightened when she did, her eyes burned, her throat swelled, so she tried to put them out of her mind. She had letters, just a few, telling her mainly of her brothers' lives. What else was her mother to say?

Blanche could not write well, and relied on neighbours, or Mr McIver, to put the words down. Could she pour out her anguish and her love, her worries and her heartbreak to them? She didn't have the words. So she told Daisy of the animals and the crops, in stiff, short sentences. She said that Eugene and Aidan were well. Of Bertie and Charlie she said nothing. She knew nothing, other than they were fighting in another country. Or dead.

She'd heard of another mother, a Mrs Pearse. Blanche had been brought up a Protestant, a British subject, and had accepted both as fact, the only way, the right way. That much was clear, and was not to take up any of her thought. Rebels were bad. Irish Republicanism was bad. Clear as day. But all such beliefs blurred now, as Blanche heard of those rebel sons, executed after the Rising along with so many others. She grieved for those boys as if they were her own. She poured all the mourning for young Des that she had stored away, all the terror for her soldier sons she'd kept in abeyance, she poured it all into grief for another mother. And still she hid it away.

February, 1917, and Daisy's pains started. Mary Ann, efficient and calm as ever, stripped the double bed of all but its mattress, and laid out newspapers on it. She'd been saving them ever since her boy had come home with his little bride. Well, she couldn't afford a new mattress, could she? Scrubbing was all very well, but the brown stains and the metallic smell never truly went away. Not after a birthing. The old sheets didn't matter so much.

Daisy did as she was told. She drank the sweet tea, she dressed in her late father-in-law's voluminous nightshirt, she lay down on the bed and she waited. She stifled the groans that spilled from her at each tensing of her womb, not sure what was to come. When the midwife arrived – or so she called herself – Daisy lay, fearful, as the brusque woman pressed and prodded.

'A long time to go yet, Mary Ann. I'll come back later,' she said.

Not a word to Daisy. Not a word of comfort or reassurance, or of forewarning. And so she left, leaving Mary Ann to explain.

Daisy knew the mechanics of it, of course. Hadn't she seen the cows, the ewes, the bitches give birth? But the pain - she hadn't expected the pain. Not like this. Floods of it, building to a climax she thought must surely render her unconscious, and then – an ebbing, a slowing, allowing her to prepare for the next onslaught.

She had not talked to Mary Ann about her own thoughts on becoming a mother. Nor to anyone. Fred? On his brief leave visits, when time was so precious, when all must be cheerfulness, no mention of war and maiming and death? Was she to voice her silly worries to him then? Or to George, that man-about-town, full of joie-de-vivre, living in the town and all set to move away to a new life in America? No, certainly not George. There was no-one. Except Bill. To him, she poured out her excitement, her mental pictures of wheeling the little one through the village, wearing bonnets and matinee coats she had made herself; she told him of her growing feelings towards the tiny person, faceless as yet, she carried inside her. And she told him of her fears. Would she be enough? Would she love this child? Would she be a proper mother? Bill said not a word, but that didn't matter.

The midwife appeared in the doorway, carrying a large funnel and some rubber tubing. Mary Ann followed her, the jug from the washstand in her hands.

'Turn onto your side, there's a good girl.' Gentler now.

Daisy did as she was told. She felt the tube being forced inside, her body's natural resistance overcome by the remorseless shoving. Then, the gushing and swilling of water, warm, soapy, as it poured into her, filling her, making her want to vomit.

'Hold it there, bach. Don't open your bowels yet.'

She was pulled from the bed, sat on the commode chair, nightdress pulled up around her waist, as the soiled liquid poured from her, splashing into the ceramic pot beneath. Twice she was told to hold it, as one pot was replaced with another. Twice she failed, as the watery contents of her bowels continued to stream onto the protective sheets placed on the floor around her. Amid the pain of her contractions, the churning of her stomach, the stinging in her rump, Daisy's overriding emotion was one of mortification. To be seen like this! By her mother-in-law – and by a stranger! She thought she would not bear it, as she was helped once more up onto the bed. One leg over the midwife's shoulder now, and no time to think – just an overwhelming urge to push her baby into the world. She groaned - low, visceral sounds - as each pain built upon the last, until an agony like no other pushed out a tiny head, and a still greater one allowed little shoulders to escape, a small body to slither, wet and warm, onto her leg, and it was done. Daisy was a mother.

1919

The war ended at last and Fred was coming home. The time between the armistice in the November, and meeting him off the boat in Swansea docks, felt like an eternity for Daisy. She stood, watching the waters lap a harbour wall as she had once before, but now with a struggling infant in her arms. She wouldn't believe it till she saw him. The Battalion known as the Swansea Pals - a thousand or more men from Swansea and the surrounds - had found themselves in the deadly battle of Mametz Wood. By 1918, more than half had given their lives for King and Country. So no, Daisy wouldn't believe it till she saw him.

She turned to her mother-in-law.

'D'you think ...' but her voice died away, as both women strained to see a speck on the horizon.

The older woman's voice seemed aimed at the ripples and the swell in front of them.

'They're being released bit by bit, they say. Not all at once. Makes sense, I suppose. But what's he supposed to do? For work? He didn't have a job before he went, for God's sake!'

Daisy could hear Mary Ann's frustration bubbling to the surface again. As always, it had the effect of quelling her own.

'Well, there's plenty of building work, goodness knows!'

It didn't seem strange to Daisy that she now saw the blitzed and battered town as her own, after living there for just two years. It was home now.

'Or the pit,' said Mary Ann.

'Aye, there's always the pit.'

They fell into their silent reveries, while little Caitlin fussed and babbled. Then, 'There it is! The boat! There!'

It was an age. Interminable. How slowly could a ship move? Inch by inch, it seemed. Time was spinning away, while the hulk nudged closer - and now there was a floating sea of faces above it, some battered, bruised, all grinning, some weeping. And then Fred was running to them, eyes crinkled, laughing, circling his three girls with his sturdy arms, and all was well.

Motherhood came naturally to Daisy. She gave hardly a thought to the old dreams, of studying, of becoming a nurse, or a vet: those were hopes for a new generation. Her role was laid out for her and on the whole, she was content. Her feelings for Fred had grown, from the adolescent excitement she had felt in the barn back home, to a settled and comfortable feeling of affection. And yes, love.

They rowed sometimes. Daisy's temper was as rich as her mothers, and she didn't give an inch.

'I'm warning you, Fred Hughes, if you come in here rolling drunk one more time, I'll be lathering you!'

'Aww come on Daise!' he'd say, stooping to give her a peck on the cheek. 'It's just a glass with the boys! No harm, Cariad!'

'I'll give you no harm! I'll not have the neighbours thinking ...'

And he'd stoop down and lift her up in his strong arms and hug her, and kiss her on the lips, and she'd laugh.

She would laugh, too, when Fred mixed up his words as he often did, although not unkindly. Terracotta he'd say, instead of instead of terra firma. They'd laugh at his silly jokes, gleaned from his workmates, often too bawdy for his mother's ears. And they would dance to the gramophone as they played Pretty Baby and Dixieland Blues when Ann Marie was out, Bill watching silently, little Caitlin gurgling with pleasure.

But news from Tobergell was bad. Soldiers returning from the front had brought with them the dreaded Spanish 'flu. Whole families were struck down, and Ireland suffered the worst. Dublin was a city cut in two, the wealthy living on the edges of town in tiered properties with plumbing and indoor toilets, while the rest lived in slums, sometimes twelve to a room, with little food, little warmth, and no sanitation. Panicked citizens succumbed to fear and profiteering, clinging to hope of prevention or cure by camphor and onions, government approved. Special wards were set up in the large hospitals to cater specifically for pregnant women who showed symptoms, exhausted nurses doing all they could for malnourished would-be mothers and their unborn babies, many of whom would not survive. And all the while, a war raging, simmering, a centuries-long struggle for control of Ireland by the Irish, not quenched by another that tore the world apart.

The letter from Mr McIver arrived on the day Daisy was about to tell Fred there was another baby on the way.

Dear Daisy

Your dear mother is too distressed to put into words the news I must pass on to you. Your brother Aidan, having travelled to Dublin to work in the munitions factory, became ill with the gripe and was taken to the hospital. He was looked after well by the nurses, but the poor boy died on October 1st.

A young man named Michael Byrne helps Eugene. Your Ma and Da are grateful for his help, and for another presence around a deserted table.

I am sorry to give you such wretched news, but it is best you know the state of things here. Do not try to visit, as the flu is rife, even in the countryside. I hope you and your family are well.

Yours
John McIver

New life and a new death. How could Daisy celebrate one while grieving for the other? But distance was a buffer. Barely two years since she'd seen her brothers, her mother, father, and yet their faces were growing dim in her mind. So she told Fred about her condition, and laughed as he hugged her gently, and she popped the letter into her apron pocket.

Daisy was a Hughes now, and not a day went by when one of the family didn't remind her of it. She was regaled with stories of the past, ancestors she got to know as kin, their histories becoming her own. She listened to the story of how the parents of Joseph, her late father-in-law, had lived in a shack in Greenhill down on the wharfs, a place known as Little Ireland, while he worked as a labouring builder and his wife scrubbed sheets for the gentry.

'A rough place it was too, by all accounts,' Mary Ann told her. 'Full of women and boys and girls, breaking up the copper ore with hammers. Buckers, they were called. Filthy they were, too,' she said, getting into her stride now. 'No, not with their habits – though some were no better than they ought to be. No, it was the powder of the ore, greenish, yellowish. It covered their clothes, got into their skin. Filthy.'

Five years they had lived in that shack, and Joe's mother prayed every day that they could leave, move away from the strange women who held a pipe between their rotting teeth, who wore old coats buttoned up to the neck to protect any decent clothing, as they loaded small lumps of ore into wheelbarrows. Five years it took for Joe's father and the other men to build the little string of terraced houses that would become Crispin Row. Five years of back-breaking work for the men, but five years of saving too. Joseph's father was one of the lucky ones. He'd taken up the offer of down-payment on a house in exchange for a large chunk of his weekly wage, so that by the time the row was finished, he owned at least part of one of them. Joseph and his siblings grew up in that elite group of Swansea residents –

they were homeowners. When Joseph married Mary Ann, they too moved in to the family home, for where else would they go?

The couple soon welcomed three boys into their lives and the home they shared with Joe's parents. William, clever and serious, head down, a thinker. Then George, a charmer even then, smiling his way into everyone's hearts. Little Alfred was still a babe in arms when a knock on the door one morning signalled the end of the life the couple had planned for their family.

Mary Ann sat by Joe's hospital bed for six days, the boys cared for by their grandparents. She held one or other of her husband's hands as best she could, obscured as they were with tubes. She wiped his forehead, talked to him, told him what was happening. And all that time he remained unconscious.

His workmates told Mary Ann what had happened. Joseph had been inspecting the work on a first-floor window from his ladder. He was careful, he knew what to do, had done it a hundred times or more. But not so the apprentice working above him on the roof. Someone should have seen that the coping stone was too big for him, too heavy. When it fell, it was fast and lethal. Joseph would never have seen it coming. It knocked him to the ground, pinning him there.

The doctors did all they could, but it was hopeless. Joseph was alive, just. Both legs would need to be amputated. It was left to Mary Ann to tell him. When he woke. But he didn't wake.

1926

Daisy and Mary Ann came to an accommodation, an unspoken one, but a binding one nevertheless. And when Mary Ann became ill with a racking cough, sometimes bringing up blood, Daisy nursed her.

'Don't fuss, Daisy!' Mary Ann complained, even as she allowed herself to be changed into a clean nightdress.

'It's a bit of a rest I need, that's all.' And she slept.

Their roles were reversed now, Daisy in charge, but she showed Fred's mother all the care and affection she would have shown her own mother, had she been able to. Her two little girls played quietly in a corner of the bedroom, while Daisy ran between the rooms, cleaning, cooking, never leaving her charges for long.

Fred pounded the streets, looking for a day's work, as a general strike took hold across the country. Food was scarce. Daisy sometimes thought of taking her family and going home. Yes, in her desperate times, Ireland was still home. But as she read the letters from Tobergell, telling of the changes in her country, she knew even that had become an impossible hope. So Daisy nursed Mary Ann till the end, talked to her, listened to her. Heard the old stories, pretended they were new. She held the older woman's hand, and promised that Bill would always have a home with her and Fred. That she'd never leave him alone.

CHAPTER SEVEN

WALES

1942

SWANSEA

No, Caitlin wouldn't understand. Indeed, Daisy didn't understand herself. Just a powerful feeling of maintaining the status quo, being respectable. She had built a life here, a place in local society. And welcoming though it was, society could be harsh. Woe betide those who strayed! So she refused Meg a home, and watched as the girl walked away.

Caitlin was the only one to visit her sister. The girl was wretched, and barely roused herself from her bed. As the months went on, still Meg lay, weeping, mourning. Caitlin found it hard to understand that level of grief. Did her sister love the man so very much? Is that what love is supposed to do to you? Caitlin tried to compare it with her feelings for Evan. She couldn't. And she watched with a kind of envy as she saw the belly swell, the breasts become plump, as she hid the secret she carried inside her.

Meg's baby was born with no fuss. Mean and meagre the area might be, but the solidarity of motherhood was strong, so a child from Dogs Lane was sent by its mother to tell Daisy of her grandchild's arrival. Daisy was reluctant, but agreed to accompany Caitlin to the apartment. They trudged through the slush and the sleet, heads down. And what she saw horrified her. Horror at the neglected appearance of the street and the rooming house, the drunken Noels issuing from the pub. Then the clutter and filth on the stairs, the mounds of soiled bedlinen in the room, the unkempt state of her daughter. But the greatest horror was directed at herself, for allowing this to happen. She saw the tiny child, asleep in a chest drawer, mewling as it slept.

'It's time you came home, lass,' she said gently

Caitlin set off the next morning with Evan in his Morris Eight, blankets piled on the back seat. She was excited. Relieved. Her sister was coming home, and her mother would care for her and her baby, and all would be well. And Meg would be home again where she belonged, and there would be a cousin for her own little one when it came. She touched her belly lightly as they drove across town. If she were right in her calculations ... Caitlin smiled to herself.

She knew something was not right. The baby's feeble whimpering, the stench of vomit, all too clear from outside the half-open door. No need to knock. No imagination needed to know what had happened. The pill box, the empty gin bottle, the lifeless body, head hanging down, a trickle of phlegm from the gaping mouth, all made a macabre and sickly pageant.

Caitlin stood in the doorway, her hands covering her mouth. She started to shake, as she retched, choked, swayed. Evan, standing behind her, dropped the armful of bedding and held her.

'Go outside, love,' he said. 'Wait for me there.'

But Caitlin walked to the bed. She moved her sister's head, gently, ever so gently, onto the pillow;

she closed her lips, then her eyes, and she pulled the counterpane over Meg's thin body. Then she bent and picked up the child, sticky in its own dirt. Evan handed her a clean blanket. She wrapped the baby, and held it to her as she wept, kissing its warm head and its matted hair, murmuring words of comfort and sorrow and love.

'Don't fret, Cariad. I'll be your mother now.'

CHAPTER EIGHT
IRELAND
1942

No-one questioned her. No-one bothered her. She was just a woman, alone, with a baby wrapped up Welsh-fashion against the spray of the Irish sea, standing in the bow of the ship, a figurehead, staring at the greyness. The taste of salt on her tongue was strong.

Did she have a plan? She didn't think so. She only knew she needed to get away from the sight and the smell of alcohol and vomit and putrefaction, to escape the questions that were bound to come, the answers she didn't have, to take the babe before someone else did.

Evan had followed Caitlin's instructions to the letter. Took her home, helped her to pack, helped put a story together. And those neighbours, those rough-and-ready souls who knew exactly what was going on, who stood together to protect what they saw as one of their own, they nodded to Evan and shook their heads to anyone who asked - baby? What baby? No, no baby here. They'd been mistaken.

It was as she'd stood cradling the little mite, her head turned from her sister's corpse, from the lips that were turning blue and the jaw that had fallen open, that Caitlin knew her pregnancy was over. Was she ever pregnant? Had it been wishful thinking? Was the warm liquid that trickled down her leg all that was left of a baby that was never meant to be, or simply her monthlies, delayed?

Evan was left to tell Daisy what her eldest daughter had done. Or at least, part of it. Not the part about taking her new-born niece. Just that she'd fled, not able to come to terms with her sister's death. And now Caitlin stood as Dublin came in sight, and she knew she needed a plan. She bent to kiss the baby's head – sweet-smelling and fluffy-haired now – as she heard an anxious Irish lilt call out, 'Mirna! Mirna, no hiding now! We're almost there!' A small child came running, giggling, from behind some drum-kegs near the railings, and her mother caught her, hugging and scolding together. Caitlin smiled.

'She's a bold one, this!' the young woman said, looking harassed. 'I need to have eyes in the back of me head!'

'She has a lovely name,' said Caitlin. 'I haven't heard it before.'

'Siobhan? Yes, it's nice enough!'

'Oh – no, I thought you called her Mirna. I'm sorry …'

The other woman laughed.

'Oh God bless you! No, that's just what I call her! Mirna's just a pet name, a baby name. I use it when I'm singing her to sleep – or when she runs off and scares the daylights out of me!'

The pair hurried off, hand in hand. Caitlin looked down at the tiny new-born's face with its huge eyes, blinking in the sunlight now, snuggled against her chest, and felt again the overpowering feeling of tenderness for this child that she had experienced since she'd first held her.

'Well, sweetheart,' Caitlin whispered, 'You need to have a name, don't you? How about Mirna?'

It took her seven hours to reach her grandmother's house, by a combination of trains and buses and helpful farmers in rusting jalopies or creaking carts. It was a fractious time. What did she know about babies? Feeding them, cleaning them, nursing them?

The bottles and nappies and creams in her hold-all had somehow been procured by Evan as he drove her to the docks. Milk too. How he had laid his hands on the new dried baby milk, Caitlin didn't ask, didn't care, but thank God he had. And she thanked God every time a fellow traveller, or a wife in a roadside farm-shop, or a tram driver, heated up the water for her to make up a feed.

She was grubby and crumpled, her eyes stinging from lack of sleep, her feet blistered from the too-tight shoes she'd grabbed in her rush to leave, when at last she and Mirna arrived.

So this was Tobergell. A village from another time. Another century, it seemed. The sun was sinking low now, and the little cottages around her took on a sheen of gold, set within their emerald surroundings. Some faint bleating was the only sound she could hear, and Caitlin felt as if she'd wandered into a nineteenth-century painting.

She walked to what seemed to be the oldest of the dwellings, and stood, clutching her baby and her bags, looking at the tiny homestead in front of her. So this was where her mother had been born. This was the place her mother had talked about so often, so lovingly, and so longingly. This was where her parents had met.

The sturdy grey stone was weathered to a silver gloss, the door was painted a cheerful yellow, and the path leading to it was clean and well swept. On either side of it, the apron of land was well-tended, preparing for the stocks and hollyhocks and roses that were soon to bloom. The sweet scents of grass and lavender and rosemary were overpowering, cleansing, and, gently, they took away the stench of birth and death that had haunted Caitlin for the past two days.

The door opened without warning.

'About time too, my girl!'

Blanche stood with her feet planted firmly on her doorstep, hands on her wide hips. Her snow-white hair was pulled into a low bun; soft skin rumpled on her round open face, but her sapphire eyes showed no signs of aging. Her smile belied the fierceness of her welcoming words.

'Come to me arms, me clump o'turf!'

And the little woman held out her arms and took Caitlin into them, and Caitlin was laughing and sobbing, and breathing as she'd almost forgotten how. She could hear her mother's voice and the childish endearment in the grandmother she'd never met, and she knew she had done the right thing in running here.

'How did you know, Gran?' she said, dabbing at her eyes as they walked into the house. 'How did you know I was coming?'

'Well now, we do have telephones you know, even out here in the backwaters!'

'Oh of course. What … what did my mam say, exactly?'

She was home. The chatting and the laughter and the banter at mealtimes, all the things she'd missed without knowing, they were all here. This was the table, she thought. The one her mother had laid, had scrubbed, had eaten from. And these were her family. Uncle Eugene with the twisted leg, just as her mother had described him. Except that in her stories, he was one of five strapping young boys, loud and strong, with boots clattering on the flagstone floor as they came in from the fields. But the kitchen, the house, the land – here was no solemn mausoleum. Eugene might be in his fifties now, but he seemed as full of life as ever he must have been. His wife Bridget was a quiet gentle soul, but Blanche soon let Caitlin know that the girl could more than hold her own if her husband stepped out of line. Their daughters, though they teased him mercilessly, clearly worshipped their father.

'Teenagers!' muttered Blanche as she passed the crockery to Caitlin to dry. 'More trouble than they're worth! Never like that in my day!' But her smile gave lie to her words, as she tutted at her granddaughters and they hugged her as they went out, laughing..

'Never thought Eugene would marry, never mind have young of his own.' Blanche put the tea-towel down and sat in her wooden chair next to the range. Caitlin was only too eager to hear more. She glanced at the crib where Mirna slept, and she perched on the settle to listen.

'He was nearing forty when he met Bridget. How he did that, God only knows! He never went out, never went drinking like the other boys of the village Never went dancing, of course, not with his leg. But suddenly there she was! Part of our lives! And how he changed, poor lamb. She really brought him out of himself. Took him to the pub, even to the Cèilidh. He – he blossomed.' Blanche drew a rough hand across her eyes. 'Yes, he's one to be proud of! And he's a good father to those girls. Soft as butter he is, but a good father.'

Caitlin saw her grandmother's eyes flicker to the row of photographs displayed in cheap but highly-polished frames, standing proud on the mantel. She knew who they were now.

'Tell me about Grampa, Gran,' she said gently.

Blanche turned, smiling.

'Another time, m'chicken,' she said. 'You're not rushing away, now are you!'

No, Caitlin wasn't planning on rushing anywhere. There was a kind of peace amongst this rowdy little crowd. There was Uncle Bertie, or 'Poor Bertie' as he was known. Shell shock, they called it. Just as Uncle Bill had suffered, so had her mother's brother.

In the same war, on the same side, just five years and the Irish sea had separated them until they found common ground on the Somme. Now he too sat, seeing only the horror in his head, hearing only the cries of young men, the sound of artillery shells and the stream of machine gun fire.

Cousins Shelagh, Eileen and Maeve were younger than Caitlin was, still in their early teens and full of fun, doting on little Mirna. All three had the copper-coloured hair of her mother, and the sapphire blue eyes of her gran. Her cousins' sisterly squabbling sometimes brought a lump to her throat but Caitlin continued to push Meg from her thoughts, stifle the grief, choke back the tears, afraid they would overwhelm her if she let them in.

The thought terrified her. The idea of losing control was one that kept her awake at night; when she did reluctantly fall into a sleep, her dreams were full of wailing, weeping, screaming; of scenes of blood and vomit and her sister's voice whispering,

'She's mine. You stole her. She's mine.' So Caitlin didn't sleep.

Caitlin listened as her grandmother spoke on the telephone. She could hear Daisy's angry, worried voice from the other end of the room, but Blanche calmed her daughter, first with soft tones, then with the sharp-tongued ones she knew Daisy would remember. The voice a hundred miles away became softer.

'Your mammy will quieten soon enough, child,' said Blanche as the conversation ended and the receiver was replaced. 'You can't blame her for blowing off steam now, can you? Her youngest going that way, poor little soul, along with her first grandchild …' She paused. 'Then her first-born skedaddling off!'

Blanche looked down into the bowl of soapy water standing in the Belfast sink as she passed the clean crockery to be dried. Caitlin took the plate from her without a word, and Blanche allowed her words to sink in, before she spoke again.

'Anyway, she says you're to stay here as long as you need. Or as long as I'm willing to put up with you! She also said Evan's doing alright, popping in every day to see if there's any news …'

Caitlin said nothing. She realised that she hadn't given her husband any thought since she had left, save for gratitude for his help. Guilt bubbled up, adding to the turmoil swirling in her head.

Blanche tipped out the water and watched it as it gurgled away. Her face was still, distant, and Caitlin could not help but wonder if her grandmother, in that moment, thought of all the dishes, all the conversations, all the years … Blanche turned, smoothed her apron, and smiled as she said,

'I've an errand for you, Cait. You can take the men their sandwiches if you would. They'll be in the bottom field by now, I'm thinking, so you can't miss them.

Bláth Farm had grown since Daisy had left it. Two more fields, a few more cattle, and a sizeable flock of sheep graced it; the vegetable garden was now a sizeable allotment, and the old barn had been joined by two more. Caitlin made her way in the direction her grandmother had pointed, grateful for the old boots she'd been loaned, as she squelched through the mud and manure, watching every footstep. She'd been reluctant to leave Mirna, but Blanche had assured her that the babe would be fine, and that some fresh air would do Caitlin good.

Caitlin heard again her grandmother's words, '… her youngest going that way along with her grandchild …' and wondered what Evan had told her mother. Had he stuck to his word? She desperately wanted to know, but was afraid to ask. And how would she ask anyway? How would she find the words she needed, to reassure herself, or dash her plans? Mirna. Mirna was hers. She would not give her up. She trudged on, head down, breathing the sweet grass-filled air, until the wooden five-bar gate stopped her progress. She looked up. And what she saw sent all other thoughts from her mind.

The green was everywhere. She realised that, as she had travelled up-country from Dublin, she had seen, but not taken in, the island's extraordinary emerald-coloured vegetation, found nowhere else.

Caitlin looked down on a carpet of jade and olive and forest green that covered the gentle slope that fell away in an early springtime haze. Hedgerows of hawthorn and blackthorn, hazel and birch, crab apple, wild cherry and holly enclosed the pastures where the sleek black cattle lazed and the fat white sheep grazed, heavy with young. Clumps of yellow furze sprouted indiscriminately in the distance, a colour contrast that highlighted the thousand shades of green. No painting would ever do the scene justice.

In the distance, in what Caitlin took to be the bottom field, she could see figures moving, and she squinted to pick out her uncle Eugene. She smiled as she imagined her mother here, all those years ago – a girl younger than she was now, and Eugene a fine young man, alongside his brothers, and she felt a stab of grief for the uncles she had not known.

Caitlin opened the gate and walked through, carefully closing it behind her. She started to walk down the field, clutching the basket of chunks of bread, cheese wrapped in fat-soaked muslin, and a hock of ham. The pitcher of ale stood upright beside this feast, and Caitlin kept an eye on it lest it tipped, as she navigated the clods of earth beneath her feet, glancing up only now and then.

Was it the effect of the spectacular surroundings that made her gasp when she saw him? Or the suddenness of him? Without warning, he was there, standing before her, broad and sweating, tawny hair tied back, sleeves rolled up past his elbows, and corduroy britches held high by canvas braces. He was smiling.

'Ah! Now here's vision!' he said, his southern-Irish accent strange to her ears.

Caitlin flushed, embarrassed, before she saw he was referring to the picnic, and she blushed to the roots. She felt unreasonably irritated, and drew herself up as tall as she could, shaking back her hair, tangled as it was in the breeze.

'Yes,' she said coldly. 'My grandmother asked me to bring the lunches down. For my Uncle Eugene and the men.'

He didn't seem to notice the frostiness in her manner.

'Your grandmother is it? So you must be Caitlin. Hello,' he said, still smiling as he held out his hand. 'I'm Michael. Mick Byrne.'

CHAPTER NINE

WALES

1942

SWANSEA

This wasn't a role he relished.

Evan was used to hiding the truth of course. It was part of his job. But in his personal life? No, this was not a comfortable situation to be in. His well-ordered mind kept the two parts of his life strictly separate - different files, different rooms. No-one questioned his version of a reserved occupation being that of a bomb-maker. A crude description, he knew, but one that would not invite questions or speculation. His qualification as an engineer he needn't mention. Recruited to the security service during his final year at Cambridge, he had felt fortunate that his posting after graduation was near his home town. MI5 was spoken of in hushed tones under its cloak of secrecy. It acquired many additional responsibilities during the war, and its strict counter-espionage role became blurred, acquiring a much more political function, involving the surveillance not merely of foreign agents, but also of pacifist and anti-conscription organisations. And they could be found anywhere. Why not in South Wales?

His place within the War Office was more subtle than that of an arsenal mechanic, and not easily understood, or indeed would be accepted. But someone had to do it. He may not carry a gun, but he was part of the war effort too.

Standing in that room, seeing Meg's lifeless body, the death mask that bore little resemblance to the girl that had been, Evan had been shocked by his own emotions. He had wanted to run, to puke, to shudder in horror at the scene, but he did none of these. He summoned his training; his unerring instinct for an operative on the wrong side of the fence, and his steely determination to turn them or take them in, came into play in this most unlikely of circumstances. All this had been hidden from

Caitlin, as it must, but now was the time for clear thinking.

He stood, gripping the door frame, holding the blanket that was to be a welcome-home gift, his face still, as he watched Caitlin arrange her sister in her bed, as she covered the thin body, as she picked up the child ...

He handed the blanket to his wife.

'Go outside, love,' he had said. 'Leave it to me.'

He didn't have much time. The doctor would have been called, by ... who? Who would have called a doctor? A neighbour? Maybe. Evan scooped up the sodden bedding and rammed it into a pillow-slip along with the pill box and the gin bottle, both empty. He ran down the stairs and saw Caitlin sitting on the back seat of their car, head down, rocking the babe in her arms. He could only guess at her thoughts, her plans - if she had any. So guess he did.

Evan opened the passenger door and dropped his linen bundle with its evidence onto the seat. Suicide was not only a shameful thing - it was against the law. No judge's ruling could hurt Meg now, he knew, but the judgement of the community would only add to the anguish her family would be feeling. He rapped, hard, on the nearest street door.

'Hello, Mrs …?'

'Sullivan, love. Brenda Sullivan.'

'Mrs Sullivan, I'm …'

"I know who you are, love. Least, I know you're something to do that little mite up the way.'

'Yes, I'm …' He made a decision. He'd be as straight with her as he could be.'

'I'm her brother-in-law. She's very unwell. VERY unwell. And she needs a doctor. Could you call one?' He rummaged in his back pocket. 'Here's fourpence.'

Brenda Sullivan nodded, took the coins, and started down the street. Evan looked once more at his wife, and recalled her words, 'I'll be your mother now.' He ran after Brenda Sullivan.

'There's no baby, Mrs Sullivan,' he said quietly. 'Never was.'

He saw her glance back into the car window. Then she nodded again.

'No baby. No, no baby.' And she marched away.

The doctor saw only what he was shown. A young woman, emaciated, extreme loss of blood. A word from Evan, with a whispered dropping of a well-regarded, high-ranking local magistrate's name, and the death certificate was signed. Cause of death - major haemorrhage, due to severe malnutrition

And then - a hurried drive home to pack some essentials, to the shops to buy a few more; a rush to the docks, and a wave farewell to a mother and child standing in the bow of the boat, as it slipped out into the Bristol Channel on its journey. All accomplished in just a few hours. But the hardest was yet to come.

Fred was inconsolable. Imprisoned as he now was in his bed, gasping for air night and day, he was stricken. His little Meg, his baby girl, gone! He had never understood why she had left home, or indeed why she hadn't come back. He hadn't questioned his wife. He trusted her. These were women's matters, no place for a man to be putting his size nines in, and no doubt Daisy always acted for the best. But now he wept, shoulders heaving in painful sobs wrenched from him.

Daisy, however, was stoical. Stony faced. Evan told her as gently as he could - that Meg had passed away peacefully, as had the babe. That there was nothing to be done, that she had known her mother loved her and had wanted her to come home. Evan did not flinch at lies such as these - they were a kindness, and nothing was to be achieved with the telling of the truth.

His training had taught him to assess all risk factors, and he weighed up the possibilities - that Mrs Sullivan would somehow pass on the information that there had been no child; or that she had seen a woman, sitting in a car, nursing a newborn. And he decided the chances were slim enough to take the chance. The woman did not mix in the same circles as Daisy; communication between them was unlikely. So Daisy and Fred would be able to arrange the funeral of their daughter, accepting that their tiny granddaughter would be in the same sealed coffin. Details of early death were not discussed with neighbours - it was unseemly, and encroached on family grief, so there would be no more said.

It was when Evan told them that Caitlin had gone to Ireland, to her grandmother, that Daisy's composure cracked. Her face crumpled and tears squeezed down her cheeks.

'But why? I need her here! Why would she go?'

Evan had his answer ready. It was one he had perfected as he drove throughout the morning, and one Caitlin had agreed to.

'Catlin was in shock, Daisy. She couldn't cope. She had to get away. She may not have told you, but she - we - are expecting a baby soon too, and what has happened to Meg was just too much for her.'

There. The lie was told, the plan put in place. Evan returned to the empty rooms above the baker's shop, alone. As he sat in front of an empty grate, he put his head in his hands.

CHAPTER TEN
IRELAND
1942

TOBERGELL

It was clear that Michael was held in high regard at the farm.

'I don't know what we'd have done without him,' Blanche told Caitlin as they cleaned the vegetables for the evening's stew. 'It was a dark time. You'd have been just a babby, over there, across the water. My youngest, Aidan - dead. I'd already lost Des and Charlie and I didn't know where Bertie was. It was just Eugene and me …'

'And Grampa? Wasn't he here?'

Blanche put her cloth down, looked up, sighed.

'Your Grampa Ambrose never got over not being able to fight. He saw it as a test of his manhood, his rite of passage if you will. He was just past the age, of course, that's why he couldn't go, but that didn't matter. He watched his sons going to war, and it made him bitter. I wish to God …'

She took up the paring knife and bent her head to her work.

'Anyway, he wasn't fit to run the farm after that. And when your Ma left ... well ... he just shrivelled. Didn't seem to care about anything or anyone. It hurt,' Blanche said simply.

'How did you manage, Gran?'

Blanche lowered herself onto the nearby bench.

'One day a young man passed through, said he'd been here before. I didn't remember him, but he was looking for work, and we needed someone – Eugene couldn't do everything, poor lamb! So Michael stayed. Worth his weight in gold, that one! He and Eugene are like brothers, though Mick's a lot younger of course. I'm glad you met him.'

Caitlin took the men's food down most days after that, and found she was looking forward to doing so, even though she wouldn't have admitted it. Mick would amble up to the gate when he saw her, and walk with her as she crossed the fields. She could not maintain her haughty demeanour for long, and they chatted easily. One day they were joined by a younger man, one of about her own age, and Mick introduced them.

'Connor, this is Mrs Caitlin Howells – it is Howells, isn't it?' She nodded, and Mick went on, 'I met her mother a long time ago.'

Caitlin looked up, surprised, but Mick continued with the formal introductions.

'Caitlin, this is my son, Connor Byrne.'

'Pleased to meet you, Mrs Caitlin Howells,' Connor said, with a mock bow. 'And it's Connor O'Byrne. I've decided to take the name of our sacred ancestors, which has been diminished over the years.' He glanced at his father, eyes narrowed. 'Just a single letter, but I've taken it back.' He bowed again, and strutted back down the field.

Mick and Caitlin followed him more slowly. Indeed, their walk took longer each day,

'You said you knew my mother, Michael. Did you? Really?'

'I did indeed,' he said. 'For a short while. She was very kind to me. The whole family was.' He turned then, and looked at her, puzzled. 'Has she never mentioned me then?' She shook her head.

'Hasn't she told you how she met your father, Caitlin?'

'She told me he was injured and she helped to nurse him, fell in love with him. No more details than that!'

They were in the bottom field now.

'Ask your Gran then. She'll remember.'

'Are you sure? She doesn't seem to remember meeting you before you came to help out. She thinks very highly of you, by the way.'

He laughed, and the sound sent a pleasant shiver through her.

'Oh, I think she remembers more than she lets on!'

She felt a twinge of regret when they reached the little posse of men waiting for their food.

Eugene came hobbling up, berating them good-naturedly.

'Well you two may have all the time in the world, but our bellies think our throats have been cut! What's the hold-up?'

'I'm sorry Uncle Gene, it's my fault. Too many questions, too much for me to catch up on!'

She wanted to stay. She wanted to sit by Mick while he ate; she wanted to watch him put the flask to his lips and watch the liquid stream down his throat, watch him wipe the back of his hand across his mouth … She stopped her thoughts in mid-flow, shocked at the powerful images she had conjured, and at the visceral pleasure they gave her.

'I'm off then, gents,' she said, and turned away. Her steps were quick and careless as she walked back through the fields, and she stumbled on small hillocks and tufts of grass, but she walked faster and faster, as if running from her imaginings. Her sudden emotions were completely new to her. He's an old man! She told herself. He's my mother's age! And yet his face, his body, his voice were at the forefront of her mind for the rest of the day.

Caitlin ran to Mirna as soon as she reached the house, somehow guilty that her thoughts were not with the child for the past hour, but the babe was sleeping peacefully, and Caitlin relaxed. She chatted to her grandmother while they chopped and sliced in the kitchen, but although she wanted to, she could not bring herself to ask Blanche about Mick's early visit to the farm. Her new-found feelings for the man were too raw, too close to the surface, too likely to be recognised by a blush or an embarrassed glance. And there was another reason. She wanted to keep these sensations to herself, to be examined later, perhaps at night, when she could relive the day.

* * *

'Isn't it about time that wee one was registered, Cait? You can do that in Larne, can't you?'

It was something Caitlin had been putting off for as long as she could. Stupidly, she knew. It had to be done. But so many lies to be told! She looked at her grandmother, and Blanche's shrewd eyes looked back.

'Sit down child. And tell me what's to be done.'

She knew she couldn't tell it all.

'I saw Meg, Gran. I saw Meg, and … and her dead baby …' Caitlin swallowed hard. 'I couldn't think straight. I had to run away.'

'But your mammy, Cait! Did you not think of her? Of what she would be going through?'

'I know!' Caitlin was sobbing. 'I know! It was cruel! But … but I was having a baby too, and … and Mam didn't know, and it seemed all wrong for me to have a baby when Meg's was dead, and … and …'

'Alright, Cait,' Blanche said quietly. 'Don't take on so. I'm not blaming you. I'm trying to understand.'

They sat in silence for some minutes, Caitlin's sobs quietening.

'So, where was Mirna born, Cait?'

'On the boat,' Caitlin murmured.

'On the ... dear Lord, on the boat! By yourself?'

'There was a woman,' Cait said, forcing herself to picture the mother she had met there. 'She helped. But, you see, I can't register my baby in Ireland if she was born at sea, can I? At least, I don't think so. I don't know. And I can't ask, can I? Because ... if ... then it's too late ...' and she continued to sob.

'You want to say she was born here.' Blanche's voice was gentle, but this was a statement, not a question. 'Yes, you can do that. Is that all?'

Caitlin shook her head, and her grandmother sighed.

'Well, out with it, girl!'

'I don't want the certificate to say, *father unknown*. And that's what it will say, because Evan's not here, and ...'

Blanche sighed. Another problem to sort.

'Ahh! I see. Well, perhaps Eugene could stand in for Evan. Stand at the back, you know! Although

…' Blanche's eyes looked unfocussed as she seemed to think through the problem.

'They'd know him in Larne. It would have to be Belfast. Although he would look a bit long in the tooth to have fathered a bairn just now!' and as she laughed, Caitlin felt her worry slip away, just out of sight.

It was all arranged and agreed, no more discussion. All planned. Mirna was to remain at the farmhouse with Blanche and her doting cousins; Caitlin would travel in the truck with Eugene, supposedly to sort out some officialdom in Belfast, while Mick and Connor sat in the back. It was important, Blanche had said, that the family routine be kept as normal as possible, so that no awkward questions would be asked, and Monday was the day for all three men to replenish the animal feedstock in the city.

Caitlin could feel cold fear run through her - fear of being found out for lying, for dragging her new-found family into her deception. And the fear increased as she heard her uncle's rasping cough get progressively worse as he drove. After half an hour, he stopped the truck.

'Mick,' he gasped, 'You'll have to drive.'

'We need to go back, Uncle Gene!' Caitlin said, but he shook his head.

'I'll be okay,' was all he could manage, as Mick helped him into the back of the truck and jumped up into the cabin.

'We'll just do the essentials, then head home,' Mick said, giving a sideways look at Caitlin and she knew, at that moment, that Eugene had told his friend what he had promised to do.

They drove the rest of the way in silence, arriving outside the City Hall in good time. Mick stopped the truck, and said quietly to Caitlin,

'I'll be the stand-in if that's okay with you, Caitlin. I don't think Eugene's up to it.'

Caitlin nodded, then shrank back in her seat as a head appeared through the sheeting behind her.

'I could do it!' said Connor. 'I could be the baby's daddy!' and he grinned. He seemed to take advantage of the silence, as both Caitlin and Mick turned to face him.

'She could be an O'Byrne then, couldn't she? A proper Irish name!'

'What are you talking about, Connor?' His father's voice was sharp.

'Oh, you think I don't know about all this, do you? How we're all pretending the babby was born at Tobergell, when we all know she wasn't? And how someone has to pretend to be the daddy …'

'That's enough, Connor!' said his father. 'You'll say no more, understand me?'

Connor grinned again, and shrugged.

'No matter. I know all sorts of little secrets. I'm very good at hearing things!'

And he bobbed back through the sheeting.

Mick helped Caitlin down from the truck. She was shaken by Connor's behaviour, and Mick was apologetic as they walked across to the imposing putty-coloured building.

'I don't know what gets into him, Caitlin. That was unforgiveable.'

'He … he's not much like you, Mick, is he?' Caitlin said quietly.

The drive back to the farm was uneventful. Caitlin gripped the piece of paper that legitimised Mirna as her and Evan's daughter. Mick kept his eyes on the road ahead; Eugene's coughing became worse, and Connor continued to grin.

CHAPTER ELEVEN
IRELAND
1942

Caitlin wept as she held Mirna closer than ever that evening, as relief merged with her guilt.

'I'm your mammy, Mirna. I'm your mammy,' she whispered over and over. The babe slept on, unknowing, and Caitlin listened to the soft breath, warm and sweet as it was on her cheek. What she felt for this child was more than she had ever expected. When she had picked up the little mite that day, she'd given no thought to the future, to the details, to the deceit she would embroil others in. She had given no thought to anything, other than to rescue the child from that scene of loss and pain. Evan had taken over - thank the Lord! He had realised what she had not - that the child would become theirs. And he had allowed his wife to break all sorts of laws, to abscond with her niece, to lie and lie again to her family, and all because he loved her.

Caitlin knew that. She knew she could never thank him enough for what he had done that day, and indeed what he continued to do, as messenger between herself and her parents, making sure that the lies stacked up. She would forever be grateful to him - and yet she knew she didn't love him, not the way he loved her. If she had, how could she have these feelings for Mick?

At last she had some understanding of what Meg had felt. She had tried to pretend it wasn't happening, but she could pretend no more. He had taken her arm as they crossed the busy Belfast street and guided her through the crowds on the other side, and Caitlin had felt giddy at his touch. They sat side by side in the waiting room, talking quietly, and she felt a thrill as she'd never known, just from being close to him. Yes, she'd had feelings like this before when he was near, but she had quashed them, telling herself that it was loneliness and grief she was experiencing. Today though, somehow, she acknowledged it, but just to herself. Not to him. Never to him.

As Mick stood at her side in the registrar's office, she'd glanced at him with what she hoped was an apologetic smile, and he nodded. Just nodded. It was then that she realised what an enormous thing she was asking him to do.

'And you're the father?'

'Yes, Sir.'

'Name?'

'Uhh .. Evan. Evan Howells.'

'Occupation?'

The official's head was bent, scribbling, as Mick cast a look at Caitlin.

'Engineer, Sir.'

Would they need more? Caitlin felt panicked. Had she given Mick enough information in their brief conversation while crossing that road? No, that was enough. Place of birth - Bláth Farm, Tobergell, County Antrim. Done.

* * *

Caitlin lay Mirna in the crib, and left her sleeping, the door of the bedroom ajar. She could hear the family chatting in the kitchen as they prepared supper, and she slipped out through the front door, into the mild spring air. She felt lighter, younger than she had for a long time, as her feet took her towards the gate, through it, and on to the top field.

Nothing had been planned, but she was not surprised to see Mick walking towards her. They were just a yard apart when they stopped.

'I'm an old man, Caitlin,' he said.

She could barely get her breath.

'No you're not!' she said.

'I'm your mammy's age.'

She nodded, and he took her hand.

'You're shivering.'

She nodded again, and he lifted his free hand, brushed a strand of hair from her cheek.

'Michael …'

When he kissed her, it was the softest touch she could imagine, and yet it burned through her, setting her whole body alight. She fell into him, as his arms encircled her. She felt his heartbeat, as fast as her own, as he pulled her close, urgent now, his fingers in her hair, his tongue circling her lips; she felt his hardness against her, thrilling her, making her want more ...

She didn't know how long they stood like that before he pulled away. His breath was coming fast as he held her at arms' length away from him. She wanted him. She moved towards him again, but he shook his head.

'Go into the house now, Caitlin,' he whispered. 'We've had a strange day, lots of feelings going on. We'll talk tomorrow. If you feel the same ...'

Tomorrow, and the world changed. Caitlin wondered if she were dreaming when she saw her mother sitting at the kitchen table. She tried to adjust her thoughts, to take in this new sphere she had wandered into. She'd known she'd have to face her mother at some point, but - today? Here? No, she wasn't prepared.

'Mam?' she whispered, bracing herself.

'My poor wee girl!' her mother exclaimed, and enveloped Caitlin in a tearful hug.

Blanche looked on, her face giving nothing away, while Caitlin extricated herself from her mother's hold.

'Well,' Daisy said, as she wiped her eyes in a spotless handkerchief. 'Let's see that granddaughter of mine!'

Caitlin stared at her mother. Where were the rebukes and reproofs, the accusations, the demands for explanations? How had the fiery, feisty, opinionated little woman turned into this mild and weepy soul?

'I'll fetch Mirna, shall I, Cait?' Blanche was walking past her as she spoke.

'Mirna! What a lovely name? However did you think of that?' Daisy was babbling. 'Oh glory be, there she is!' she cried, as Blanche carried the sleepy baby in.

The three generations of women sat in the homely kitchen while the child slept on, cups of tea comfortable on the scrubbed table, aromas wafting from the stew pot on the range, Blanche and Daisy making small-talk about babies and their memories. Caitlin calmed herself.

'It's lovely to see you, Mam. But … what are you doing here? I mean … did Evan not tell you … I … I'll be coming home soon …' and she felt herself flush as she said it, thinking of the reason she wanted to stay.

'Well, your Gran telephoned me,' Daisy said, 'and told me how well the bairn's doing, and thinking it might be time now …'

The telephone call the previous evening had been a hurried one, but Blanche felt she could wait no more. She had never given voice to her suspicions about what had gone on in the barn all those years ago, but she wasn't stupid. And now, it hadn't taken St Patrick to divine the way the wind was blowing with her granddaughter and Mick. She had to tell her daughter. And so she called her.

Daisy was mortified at the thought her own mother had suspected she'd slept with both young men that summer - and never said a word. She tried to explain, to tell her what had really happened, that she was young and inexperienced, comforting …fumbling … experimenting … but Blanche brushed her excuses aside.

'That's all in the past, girl. It's now I'm thinking of. Caitlin - and Michael Byrne'

'What?' Daisy whispered. 'What? No!'

And the 'phone was down, and she was gone, only to arrive at the farm on a milk wagon as the sun rose.

Now …

'Yes Mam, I will be coming home, I told you.'

'And of course, there's Evan … there's your husband … he's been very good to me, that boy …' Daisy was blethering again.

Blanche interrupted.

'Shall I take the wee one for a little walk, Caitlin?' she said. 'Give you two some time to talk?' and without waiting for a reply, she put the baby in the old pram and went out.

'Talk? What does Gran mean, Mam?'

Daisy cleared her throat. Was she nervous?

'Your gran tells me you've become friendly with Michael Byrne,' she blurted out.

'What? Well, I suppose … yes, we've got to know each other.' Was she blushing? Was the heat that crept up her neck, up her throat, into her cheeks, visible?

'A bit more than that according to her. And she doesn't miss a trick, that one. Not a trick.'

And yet, Caitlin thought, her mother didn't sound angry, as she would have expected. Just hesitant, uneasy. Before Caitlin could give any sort of reply - a denial perhaps, affronted at the implication of impropriety - Daisy carried on.

'There's something you ought to know.' Again, the clearing of the throat. Then,

'There's a chance … just a chance … that Michael Byrne might be your father.'

CHAPTER TWELVE
WALES
1953

PENYBONT

Siobhan clung fast to her mother's hand. Caitlin knew what this day meant to her daughter, knew the little girl had been waiting for it for so long, and yet, now that she was here, standing at the top of the hill, looking at the smooth path in front of her, the leather strap of her maroon fabric satchel stretched across the sturdy little body as it bounced on her hip, Caitlin could see that Siobhan wasn't so sure.

Other mothers stood around, saying goodbye, waving, scolding, kissing their children.

'Off you go then, love,' Caitlin said. 'Remember – you're my big scholar.'

And she let go of the dimpled hand.

The walk back up the hill, past the row of semis on either side of the newly-made road, gave Caitlin time to think. Time she did not want. This would be the first of many such walks, four times each day, for as long as little Siobhan was at primary school. It didn't seem that long since Mirna had started her first day here, and now she was at the grammar, catching the bus all by herself, proud of her blazer and her leather satchel and her shiny black shoes.

Caitlin forced her mind to dwell only on her daughters for as long as she could. It was rarely, now, that she thought of Rhys, their little boy, seemingly perfect in every way, but whose organs had failed him; the little boy who should have been starting in the junior school, had he lived more than a few short hours. He was the baby who would mend them, wipe away the feeling of being strangers they both had felt since she'd come home. It had taken a few years, but at last there was to be something good in their lives. But it wasn't to be.

Too soon, she was walking through the gate leading to their smart new house, too soon at her front door.

She turned the key and walked into the small, neat hallway.

'It's only me!' she sang

Just a habit, really. Who else would it be?

She walked up the stairs, her steps heavy, and into the box room where Evan lay on his single bed. No longer the handsome, well-built man she had walked down the aisle with all those years ago. Such a lot of living had been done since then. Now his body was too thin, and the parchment of skin than covered his gaunt face was drawn tight over his cheekbones, the yellowing reflected in the sclera of his eyes. He smiled at her.

'She went off okay then?' His voice was strained, painful to hear.

Caitlin sat on the bed and held his fleshless hand, the fingers bony.

'Yes, she went in like a little trouper!' she said softly.

How many times had she sat like this? The illness that recurred and recurred again and laid him low, that sucked the life from him, and her too, gave no let-up. It was three years since he'd returned from Persia. Invalided home. Glandular malaria, the docket said. He'd been treated out there, in Abadan, where he'd been sent by the war office to oversee the workers as they drilled for oil in the desert. Had he wanted to go, she sometimes wondered? Had the sound of a crying infant been something he was glad to leave? Had Caitlin's demeanour, so altered since her return from Ireland, helped his decision? He'd had no choice anyway.

What was the War Office to do with someone whose work in military intelligence had dried up? Nationalistic sentiments were on the rise in the Middle East, and they wanted their man on the ground. So they sent him - this well-dressed, clever, knowledgeable man, who was more used to a desk than an oil rig, more used to sitting on a Chesterfield chair than squatting on a concrete plinth, watching oil bubble up through the sand when the heat grew too intense.

Two years he'd been there, missing all of Siobhan's milestones. Caitlin had moved back into her parent's house, her bed-bound but beloved Pops stepping into the role vacated, unwillingly or not, by Evan.

'That's something else I've missed, Cait,' Evan whispered now. 'And Mirna - did she get off okay too? Big school?'

'Yes, she did, love.'

Caitlin stood, took the half-step that was all she needed to reach the chest of drawers, and picked up the tray. Evan groaned, and she felt a wave of tenderness for him.

'I know, I know,' she said. 'It'll be over soon.' Caitlin kept up her chatter as she prepared the needle. 'It hasn't lasted so long this time, has it? The fever. You'll be eating properly again in no time.' He allowed her to roll his ravaged body onto his side. 'And then we can think about doing the garden.'

She searched his shrunken buttocks for a patch of flesh that hadn't been punctured a hundred times. Scar tissue hardened the soft underlying muscle. She resorted, as she had before, to inflicting the hypodermic into his skinny thigh. Not a murmur. The doctor had told her that the injection of quinine into the muscle was extremely painful, but Evan never made a sound.

'It's not been so bad this time, has it?' Caitlin busied herself with tidying the tray of medicines, turning away from his frail body. She felt a deep compassion towards her husband, but the sight of his wasted body repelled her.

'The fever hasn't lasted so long,' she said again, 'and I think it's on its way out.'

She swabbed the thermometer with an alcohol wipe before shaking it and placing it carefully under his tongue. She didn't want to see his grateful eyes looking up at her; his wordless gratitude was more than she could bear, and more, she knew, than she deserved.

'Yes, it's coming down. You'll be up and about in no time!' her bracing words sounded hollow even to her, but Evan smiled.

'I love you. Cait,' he said.

'I know you do, sweetheart,' she replied.

CHAPTER THIRTEEN
PERSIA

1948

ABADAN

The heat hit him as he reached the open 'plane door, forcing him to take a step back. The light was blinding, and so it was with half-closed eyes and sweating palms that Evan arrived in the Persian city of Abadan, on the island of the same name.

A beautiful city it might have been, and perhaps it still was, if a visitor looked beyond the drilling rigs, rising like skeletal monsters across the land. Because all anyone cared about in this desert country was one thing - oil.

Oil was the source of wealth and of international trade, the cause of fighting and of wars, the leverage allowing nations to work together or the barrier that brought them to a standstill. And because of the value of its oil, countries fought over which one owned it. This was the situation in which Evan found himself, a representative of Great Britain on foreign shores.

Many, if not most, British officials believed that Persian petroleum was actually and rightly British petroleum, because it had been discovered by the British, developed and exploited by the British through their skill, their ingenuity. It was regarded as a huge overseas asset, and a source of national pride in post-war Britain. In contrast, Iranians believed the concession granted by Iran in 1933 to the Anglo-Iranian Oil Company was immoral, and indeed, illegal. The Iranian government now contested every facet of the British presence in Iran, including the British insistence on referring to the country as Persia rather than Iran.

And here he was, employed and dispatched by that very company. Tensions were taut. This city, whose population was less than that of his home town, was hostile to him in the sullen, unspoken way an offspring might treat a parent whose admonishment he felt unfair. As a British engineer, an overseer of works, Evan was referred to by the native workers by a variety of names, both Persian and Arabic. Sometimes *Arbab* and *Rayiys*, which, by the bowing of the head and the palms together, implied 'boss' or 'master', while *Ajam* may be accompanied by a sly grin under the bowed head, hinting at a more subservient title.

Evan felt uncomfortable at every level in this strange country. He may not have spoken their language, but he had sympathy for the people of this ancient place, whose land and minerals were being appropriated by others. Meanwhile he had a job to do. He was constantly reminding the men to get back to work, to stop lounging, chatting, smoking. They did so grudgingly, and only as long as he were watching them.

The only relief for Evan in this fiery outpost was a friendship he struck up with another of the engineers, another Welshman. Gilbert Williams was an old hand at this - he'd worked in Cape Town, in nearby Kuwait, and in Delhi, before he'd arrived here, a freelancer.

'I got out of Delhi before the partition. It was on the cards, of course,' he told Evan as they sat, smoking, on the veranda of one of the wooden structures that housed British officers. 'Some trouble in Kuwait, too, though I may go back there soon.'

Evan was surprised to find that Gilbert's wife Joyce and his daughters were in Abadan with him.

'She didn't trust me to come on my own!' Gilbert had laughed. 'Had a few scrapes in the past, you know!' he'd added, winking.

Evan wondered briefly what Caitlin would have made of the place, and decided that she was better off at home. He heard that Gilbert's baby daughter had been born in the local hospital, around the same time that Siobhan had arrived, and he felt the usual stab of longing for his home and his family. Caitlin had seemed more than usually distant from him since she'd returned from Ireland six years ago. At first, he put her manner down to the effect of her sister's death, and then that of their little son, but ... six years? He'd been afraid to ask in case he was the cause. So when the request came for him to be stationed abroad, he convinced himself that their relationship would improve after a little time apart, and he told her it was an order.

'How on earth do they cope, Gil?' he asked now.

'Oh, they're fine. Another year and we'll be going back home anyway - at least, for a while. I get itchy feet, don't I!'

Gilbert was happy to pass on his tips for surviving in the desert.

'Never sit directly on the ground. Or on the concrete plinths around the mess halls. You'll burn your arse off!' he laughed. 'And look out for bubbling in the sand. Sometimes it's so hot that the oil just erupts in little spurts. No rig needed!'

Evan digested the information, understanding now why Gilbert always sat on his haunches when taking a break, and he determined to squat himself in future.

They talked, too, about the future, about plans for when they were home in Wales.

'I have an idea, Ev. An idea about plastics. It's the thing of the future you know, and factories are starting to pop up all over Britain. So why not in Wales? I know there are a few, but I think a specialist one would make a lot of money. How about it?'

'I don't know anything about plastics. I told you Gil, I studied optics in uni - you know, lenses and such. We never did anything around plastics.'

'Of course you didn't! When were you studying? Late thirties? It wasn't widespread then.' Gilbert sucked on his pipe as he re-lit it. 'Nothing difficult about it really. You buy in the pellets, pour them into a machine to melt them, then into a mould. And hey presto, you've made ... well whatever you want to make!'

Evan laughed.

'I have a feeling it could be more complicated than that! But you said a specialist one.'

'Mmm …' Gilbert continued to pull on his pipe.

The first bout of malaria was a bad one. Fever, shaking, chills, headache, nausea, vomiting. Yellowing of his skin and his eyes, and severe anaemia. Evan was delirious for much of the episode, lying in the camp hospital, and when the worst of the episode was over, he was left weak and lifeless. He wasn't sorry to be shipped home as 'unfit for a desert climate.'

CHAPTER FOURTEEN
WALES
1950

Siobhan was two years old when Evan arrived back in Swansea, and she saw him as a stranger. Caitlin guessed how much it must have hurt him to see his little daughter run to his father-in-law, sick man though he was, and call him Pops, but what could she do? The child was simply imitating her mother.

The homecoming was strained; the separation had done nothing to narrow the distance between them - quite the opposite. Caitlin felt she was talking to a stranger. Evan was diffident in bed, not sure how his overtures would be received. He was not yet fully recovered, the house was over-crowded, and they had little privacy.

'Pops is taking up the parlour now,' she said in a whisper to Evan as they lay in her childhood bed, afraid to wake the toddler in her cot, or nine-year-old Mirna, asleep on a camp bed at the foot of theirs.

'His chest is so much worse, but he's hanging on. Uncle Bill is still in the middle bedroom, and Mam's in the back. Mam and I aren't on the best of terms …' Caitlin stopped. She would not talk about her return from Ireland. Would not think about it.

'So - we need to find somewhere. Quick.'

'Well …'

'Well? Well what?' she asked him, impatient.

'Well, a friend of mine - someone I met out in Persia - told me about a new housing estate being built. Nice semis. All mod cons. Garden. New school nearby …'

Caitlin sat up.

'Yes? Really? To let?'

'No. For sale.'

She lay down again.

'But … but I think I have enough for a deposit. They paid me good money for my stint in Persia. So I should be able to get a mortgage…'

More cautious now, Caitlin sat up, slowly.

'Really? Honestly? Could we?'

He smiled.

'Yes, we could.'

She kissed him them. A kiss of relief, and of gratitude. No more, he knew.

'Where is it, Ev? Is it local?'

'No. It's outside a town called Penybont, twenty-odd miles away.'

The house was perfect, built in a cul-de-sac away from the main road. Brand new, with a small lawn at the front and a bigger one at the back, with gooseberry and blackcurrant bushes, and a privet hedge separating their garden from their neighbour. A dining room, a lounge and a scullery downstairs, three bedrooms and a bathroom above. Perfect.

Caitlin walked around, examining everything, exclaiming over the tiniest detail, all her earlier misgivings about the distance from her hometown seemingly forgotten. Evan followed her, still frail, but he looked happy that he had pleased her.

'Gil has bought a house just round the corner,' he told Caitlin. 'His wife, Joyce - she's very nice. You'll like her. They have an older daughter Valerie, and a little girl Siobhan's age.'

The deal was done, the documents signed, and before they knew it, it was moving day. Their previous homes had been rented fully-furnished, so new furniture had to be bought. This was of the wartime utility variety, plain and cheap but well made, and Daisy provided the couple with linen and crockery to add to their own.

The neighbourhood was a friendly one, with young families all around them. Joyce Williams was as welcoming as Evan had hoped, and he and Caitlin settled well. Evan seemed to spend many hours locked away with Gilbert in his shed, until one evening he came home looking more alive than he had done for some time.

'We're going into business, Cait,' Evan said as he walked through the door. 'Gil and I. We're going into business. We're going to open a plastics factory!'

It was all Caitlin could do to persuade him to sit down for his supper, so excited was he. She was surprised at his news - he had never before expressed any interest in going into business, and certainly not in plastics, but it was good to see him so enthused. She questioned him while he ate his stew.

'Do you know anything about plastics, Ev? I didn't think …'

'That's the beauty of it, Cait! You don't need to know! There are machines that do all the work, you just pour pellets in and out comes whatever you want! Oh, and you need the molds of course. You can buy them. Or make them!'

He ate a mouthful of his food hurriedly, anxious to explain further.

'The plastic isn't expensive - it's made from petrol and there's plenty of that. It can be molded into any shape, any novelty you can think of.'

He gulped down a mouthful of tea.

'And what will make our factory special? We'll make lenses!'

Evan sat back, triumphant.

'Lenses, Ev?'

'Yes, lenses! Plastic lenses! Lenses for cameras, for specs, for microscopes, for magnifying glasses - all sorts! You can only get glass ones. Plastic ones will be lighter, cheaper. They won't smash. And I know about lenses!'

And so the business was set up. Gilbert seemed to know about this, which was a relief to Evan as he had no experience of manufacturing. Premises were easy to find. A huge munitions factory - crucial to the war effort, but now surplus to requirements - was practically on their doorstep, and many of the units there were vacant. They named their company Mirval, combining the names of Evan's and Gilbert's eldest daughters.

Paperwork was drawn up, machinery brought in, and it was at that point Caitlin asked, for the first time,

'Where's all the money coming from, Evan? To set this up? It must be costing a fortune!'

She had never seen Evan blush before. This was not the man she remembered, the man who had courted and wooed her, who had been her rock when her sister had died. Now he looked wary, nervous. Embarrassed? But he answered her.

'I borrowed it, Cait. From the bank. Put the house up as collateral. No, don't worry …' he added as she started to speak, 'It's all fine. We'll be making money in no time!'

She had always left their finances to her husband, as did most women. And she trusted him. But … their home?

'I see,' she said. 'And Gilbert? Is he doing the same?'

There it was again, that tinge of pink in his sallow cheeks.

'He wanted to, Cait, but the bank wouldn't cough up. He's had some falling-out with a firm in the past - all a big misunderstanding, he told me - so he's not seen as good a bet as I am.'

Caitlin said nothing. She trusted Evan. But Gilbert? She wasn't quite so sure.

But make money they did. Evan's knowledge of optics was invaluable to the business; they started to branch out, making novelty items for a local toy manufacturer, and contracts came flooding in. He was spending more and more time at the factory, regularly working eighteen hours a day, seven days a week, and eventually the strain took its toll. A relapse. His malaria resurfaced.

Caitlin had not seen Evan suffer an episode before, and she was horrified. He had not been able to warn her - after all, he was delirious for most of his illness in Abadan. But she nursed him, sponged him when he sweated, covered him when he shivered, administered his medication. His temperature rocketed, but it soon came down and within the week he was back at work - weaker, paler, but determined.

The two boys he'd employed had held the fort admirably while he was away, but there was a backlog of paperwork to catch up on, and he asked Caitlin to help. She was only too pleased to take some of the strain from his shoulders, and could easily manage some filing and letter-writing from their dining-room table while looking after the children. She didn't mind. But she had to ask.

'Evan, what's Gilbert doing all this time? Why didn't he sort this out while you were ill?'

'He's … he's not really a hands-on kind of partner, Cait,' Evan replied. 'He's better at going out and getting new contracts, that sort of thing.'

Caitlin didn't argue. She looked at his tired, drawn face, and didn't say anything more. But she wondered.

CHAPTER FIFTEEN
WALES
1942 - 1948

Caitlin's head spun as Eugene drove her to the port. She had refused to wait for Daisy, or indeed to travel with her. Images came into her head, of Michael, walking up the field that first day; of Michael standing by her at the register office; of Michael, holding her close. Then of her mother, her MOTHER, telling her that awful truth ... the horror of it all made Caitlin want to retch. Her mother, who had treated Meg like a prostitute, who had refused Meg a home, and relented too late. It was her mother who had slept with strangers - two strangers.

Caitlin's anger and disgust at her mother was tinged with something else: she felt guilt and revulsion at herself, that she could have had those feelings for a man who could be her father. And yet more self-loathing each time she saw his face in her mind's eye, because she still had those feelings for him.

'You okay?'

Eugene's voice made her start.

'Yes, I'm okay, Uncle Gene. I'm just …'

'Don't you worry your head, girl. I've seen enough family squabbles to know that sometimes the best thing to do is walk away. Walk away.' His eyes remained on the road. 'But if ever there's anything you want to talk about … well, you know where I am.'

Caitlin felt tears sting her eyes. This lovely man, who had overcome so many obstacles in his life, had welcomed her and her baby into his family without a question asked. Blanche had made them welcome too, of course, but all the time she'd suspected the truth. Known more than she'd let on. Could Caitlin forgive her?

She nodded, and Eugene patted her hand.

* * *

Evan put his wife's apparent melancholy down to reminders of her sister, now she was back home. When Daisy arrived in Swansea a few days later, it was clear that the two women had fallen out, but neither was willing to talk about it.

Much as he wanted to settle into family life, Evan found this not to be possible: Caitlin kept Mirna to herself, and kept him at a distance.

Over time, their relationship started to recover. Over time, she allowed him to make love to her. And over time, he accepted that this was how it was going to be. When Caitlin told him there was a baby on the way, he had a faint hope that things would improve. But little Rhys had died before he'd lived. And then Siobhan arrived.

For a while, their marriage seemed to improve, as they both fussed over their baby daughter, but it never rose to what he craved. He began to feel bitter towards his wife, knowing how much he had supported her when she'd needed it. And yet … he loved her dearly. It was in this frame of mind that he received the request from the War Office.

CHAPTER SIXTEEN
WALES
1956

PENYBONT

Evan's illness continued to flare up on occasion, but now they knew how to deal with it. The boys at the factory were used to Caitlin popping in to pick up the books, and they were capable to running things for a few days at a time. Caitlin knew how to care for her husband, who obediently moved into the box bedroom whenever he started to feel unwell.

But each time, he lost a little more weight. Each time, his skin took longer to regain a healthy pallor, and each time he became more frail. Between episodes of illness, he continued to work, building the business up, taking on more contracts, while Gilbert was noticeable by his absence.

Then the blow fell.

President Nasser of Egypt took over the running of the Suez Canal. Supplies of fuel from the

Middle East had been blocked. Petrol would be in short supply, and rumours of rationing were growing.

Caitlin watched her husband as he grew more anxious by the day. She could not understand why the news was affecting him so much.

'Is it the petrol rationing, Evan? Because we don't have to drive far, do we? We can manage, just staying at home …'

His face when he looked at her was stricken.

'It's oil, Cait. The oil can't get through. Plastic is made from oil, so …'

Caitlin absorbed this.

'But … it won't last forever, will it? This Suez thing? It will get sorted out, won't it?'

'Not soon enough, love. Orders are already drying up. My customers are afraid, they won't take the risk - and I can't keep the business going without them. There's no leeway, no room for manoeuvre …'

'What about Gilbert? He can help to tide things over, can't he?'

Evan's laugh held no humour.

'You haven't talked to Joyce lately have you? Gilbert's gone. Disappeared. With his secretary. It's almost funny, isn't it?'

By the time Evan's relapse was in full swing, he had paid off their creditors with the last of the paltry sum he'd received from the sale of the factory. They would lose the house now, that much was certain.

The episode of malaria that followed was the worst Caitlin had seen. The doctor told her there was little point in his being admitted to hospital, as, one by one, his organs were failing him, shutting down, and there was little that could be done. Caitlin continued to nurse him. She found it hard to believe he was not going to recover. They'd been here before, hadn't they? He'd always bounced back. Surely, surely …

'You know I'm dying, Cait, don't you?' he said to her as she prepared his medication.

She turned her back, tidying his tray, arranging pill bottles in order.

'There's no need to talk like that, Ev. It's …'

He struggled to sit up, then fell back onto his pillow.

'There's every need, Cait. There's something … something I need you to promise me.'

He waited.

'Well?' Caitlin said at last.

'Tell Mirna, Cait. Tell Mirna who she is. Tell her about her mother.'

Caitlin turned at last.

'I'm her mother, Evan.' Her voice was quiet. 'I'm her mother, and she knows exactly who she is.'

'Cait …'

'No more, Evan! No more!' Her voice cracked.

'Oh Cait, my beautiful girl.'

Evan's voice, soft, loving, gentle, was too much. She allowed the tears to fall at last, as she put her arms around the man who, she knew, had loved her all along, devotedly.

'I was so wrapped up in myself, in Mirna, I forgot about you. I'm sorry. I'm so sorry.' She cried now, her weeping full of regret and apology.

'I know, cariad, I know. You became a mother and you did what you had to do. I understood. But you must tell her, Cait. And you must tell your Mam. She deserves to know the truth. Please, Cait. Please promise me.'

Caitlin had no choice. She nodded, soundless against his shoulder.

'Such beautiful hair,' Evan said, stroking her head softly and whispering now. 'Did I ever tell you, that's the first thing I noticed about you?'

'I never told you I loved you, did I?' she said through her tears. 'I never told you how grateful I was. How much you mean to me.'

That wasn't what he needed to hear, she knew. Would it matter now? Would one more lie matter, alongside the others she had told?

'I love you, Ev. I always have.'

His smile was fragile but real as she felt his breath stutter with a final shuddering gasp.

CHAPTER SEVENTEEN
WALES
1957

Caitlin stared into the mirror and saw a face she didn't recognise. No matter. She adjusted her hat, that hat, that hated hat. Her mother's voice echoed up the stairs.

'Caitlin, are you ready? The cars are here.'

One more look around the room. Back here then. Back to where she was a girl, where she was young, where she had a sister …

'Coming.'

The big cars purred discreetly as the coffin was carried out. Another coffin. Another loss.

'I don't want to go, Mam. I don't think I can go.'

'Away with you, girl! You'll say your farewells like the rest of us. Now get in the car.'

Caitlin had already said her farewells to Pops. She had steeled herself, determined not to show him that she was broken, but she needn't have worried. One look at the frail body, lying in his bed in the parlour, gasping for air, choking, coughing, and she knew who was broken. She rallied for him.

'Well, look at you, just showing off, looking for sympathy!' she said with a smile, her voice gentle.

He smiled back.

'I know love, it's just a bit of maldod I'm after!'

A coughing spasm rasped again. She waited, smoothing his rough old hands, tracing the blueness of his veins with her finger.

'It's the dust, see,' he gasped. 'Always the dust.'

She kissed him then, as she had so many times, feeling the skin of his cheek, sunken now. And she sat with him until he slept.

Caitlin felt entirely alone. Her big strong Pops had gone, leaving a gaping hole in her life. Evan had gone, the man who had loved her unconditionally and whom she'd never truly appreciated. She had kept her promise. It was a week after his funeral that she found herself alone with Mirna who was still grieving for the man she called Daddy.

'Mirna, sweetheart, before he died, Daddy asked me to promise him something. He made me promise I'd tell you … something.' She stopped.

'Tell me something? Tell me what?' The girl hardly looked up as she lay on her bed.

'It's … it's about you. About when you were born.'

A glimmer of interest now.

'You've never told me anything about when I was born. Why now?'

'I promised Daddy.'

A wall of tension stood between them as Caitlin took a breath.

'I didn't exactly give birth to you, love.'

Mirna sat upright.

'What? What on earth does that mean?'

Another breath, and Caitlin tore the plaster off.

'My ... my sister, Meg. She had you. Gave birth to you. But she was very weak, very sick, and ... and she died.'

'What? What are you talking about, Mum?'

'I couldn't leave you there, Mirna. I couldn't. You might have been taken to an orphanage, anything. I couldn't. I ... I took you with me. I loved you, Mirna. I've always loved you.'

Caitlin stopped. No more to say.

'You took me, then? You stole me? From my mother?' Mirna whispered. 'You left my mother and took me?'

'Sweetheart, she was gone. It was too late for her ... '

'You took me?' Mirna repeated. 'What about my father? Where was he? Did he even know I existed?'

'Your father - your birth father - was killed in the war,' Caitlin said gently. 'But Daddy has been your father. And I ... '

'You!' Mirna spat the word. 'You've just told me you lied and lied all my life! All of you did! And Nanna - she lied too!'

'No, no, your Nanna didn't know. She doesn't know.'

Caitlin saw such hatred in her daughter's eyes it took her breath away. Then the girl was gone.

So here Caitlin was, back in her childhood home. The familiar trinkets and ornaments around her gave her no comfort. She felt they were mocking her, a woman touching forty, a widow, still reliant on her mother's good nature - or was it duty - to provide for her.

Their house had gone, of course, along with most of their possessions, used to pay creditors. No sympathy from them, no understanding, for a man who had died of a foreign-brought disease; no feeling for his wife and children left behind, homeless, destitute; no care for the world affairs that had brought this on them. And Gilbert? Where was he? Joyce hadn't known either.

* * *

'So he's buggered you up too, has he?'

Joyce's voice was calm as she poured tea for Caitlin. They sat at the table under the window in her living room, the table where, just a short time ago it seemed, Mirna and Valerie had sat making clothes for tiny plastic dolls out of bits and pieces of fabric, fur, lace and sequins, treasures always to be found in Joyce's scrap box.

This neat semi was a replica of every other house in the street, except that this one was full of mementos of the family's time in Persia – a beautiful pouffe with woven strips in different colour leathers; intricate carved ornaments, imposing wooden furniture, a wooden jewellery box inlaid with mother-of-pearl. Evan had brought none of these when he'd made his hasty unplanned return home.

'How do you cope, Joyce?'

'I have my brothers. They're wonderful - I've had to stop them from murdering Gil on times though! God knows why I've always taken him back - I know he's a philanderer, a con man, you name it - but he sweet-talks me round every time.'

She took a sip of tea.

'No more though, Cait. No more. He's cleaned out our savings, gone off with that slip of a girl to God-knows-where, and Pamela keeps asking where her daddy is. It's … it's just bloody cruel.'

Joyce's voice trembled for the first time.

'She's Siobhan's age, isn't she? Pamela?' said Caitlin gently.

Joyce sniffed, her composed face restored.

'Yes,' she said. 'She'll miss her little friend when you go. And no, I don't think you'll get anything from him. Gilbert. I don't think you stand a chance. I wish I'd warned you …'

* * *

The thought of that man brought a vestige of life back to Caitlin, the bitterness she felt letting her know that at least she was alive.

'Mummy? Are you upstairs?'

Thank God for Siobhan! Caitlin rubbed the back of her hand across her eyes.

'Yes love, I'm upstairs.'

It had taken a long while after their return from Ireland for Caitlin and her mother to regain a semblance of their relationship. And now, she knew, she would put that fragile connection at risk again. She had no choice. If she didn't tell her mother, then Mirna would.

Mirna had all but disappeared. Staying with a friend, she said, but who knew? Now and then she would reappear, sullen and spotty, creased and unwashed, and Caitlin had no answers to Daisy's questions.

'I'm going to look for him,' Mirna announced one morning, arriving unannounced at the door to the back kitchen, making Caitlin start.

'Oh love, are you okay? It's ... look for him? Look for who?'

'My father. Well, at least, his family. MY family! So I don't need you and your lies any more.'

The girl turned and left as suddenly as she'd arrived, leaving Caitlin shocked, speechless ... terrified. Would Mirna find Graham's family? How would they react at finding he'd had a daughter? Would they even believe her? Would she be hurt all over again? But Caitlin knew she must tell her own mother before Mirna hit out at her in the most hurtful way she could.

She heard the front door open and she braced herself.

'Caitlin? Someone here for you.'

Daisy bustled into the room, alone.

'For me? Who? Where ...?'

'I left her at the door. How am I to know if you want to see her? It's that Rosemary,' Daisy said with a sniff.

'Rosemary? Who's Rosemary?'

Daisy sighed.

'That flighty friend of yours from school! She's back in Swansea, so she says. Well, are you going to bring her in?'

'Oh, I don't know, Mam. It's been … so long. I don't know her any more. I don't think …'

'It's up to you Cait - but if you ask me, you don't have much to lose. Mebbe you could do with a friend.'

Caitlin swallowed hard. From her mother, that was an unexpected show of understanding. She walked to the door, a false smile painted on her lips, and for a second, saw a smiling, middle aged woman with short dark hair, wearing a fitted tweed suit. A split second later, she saw the cheeky young girl who was always getting into scrapes - and Caitlin burst into tears and hugged her.

'Blimey girl, don't go on so!' But Rosemary's voice was kind, and she pushed a tendril out of Caitlin's eyes, as she said, 'D'you think I can come in now? We're making a bit of an exhibition of ourselves on the doorstep!'

She had been lonely. She knew that now. And without another thought, Caitlin let all her worries and fears pour out of her, as she and her old friend sat on her and Siobhan's beds, tea growing cold as they cradled their cups, the sun dipping down outside the sash window as streetlamps were lit.

So many secrets! Locked away, stored up, always afraid of letting something slip. And the guilt. Meg, Mirna, the lies told to her grandmother. And Michael, Michael …

'You snogged your Dad? Good God Cait, that's a bit much!

At last Caitlin could breathe. The release the outpouring had given her was almost physical. She felt lightheaded, and despite herself she laughed at Rosemary's reaction.

'No! Not snogging! Well, not really ... And he's not my dad ... at least, I don't think so ... and I didn't know ...'

She sobered immediately. Rosemary reached across and briefly held her hand.

'Of course you didn't, Cait. I know. So - tell me about him.'

And she did. Caitlin hadn't ever talked about Michael, hadn't mentioned his name, let alone her feelings for him. The relief she felt now, talking to someone who was practically a stranger, was overpowering. The words gushed from her: what he looked like, how she'd met him, how he had spoken in his Irish lilt; how she'd felt each time she saw him, thought about him; how it had felt to be held by him, and how many times he'd invaded her dreams at night. And Rosemary listened.

'It's so wrong, Rose!' Caitlin said, once she had drawn breath. 'He may be my father. I don't know. No-one knows, no-one will ever know. But the thought that he could be ... and ... and the feelings I had for him ... I'm so mixed up ...'

'I don't know what to say, Cait, I really don't. I can't see a way forward, any happy ending. I'm so sorry. Does your mother know how you feel? She must be very mixed up too!'

'I think my Gran guessed there was something going on between us. And I think she'd guessed, all those years ago, that something might have gone on between him and my mother. That's why Gran called her, that's why my mother came rushing over. But we've never talked about it. I just can't.'

'I understand that, Cait. But you have another problem to sort out, don't you? Will you tell her about Mirna?'

'Oh God! Yes, I'll have to, or Mirna will. What a mess!'

A tap on the bedroom door, and both women froze.

'Caitlin?'

Her mother's voice.

'Come in, Mam,' she said. Was her voice steady?

Daisy didn't look daunting at all, standing in the doorway. Still tiny but thickening as she grew older, grey hair neat, the inevitable floral apron across her sturdy body. And yet Caitlin felt the dread of a ten-year-old, coming in late for supper.

'Why don't you girls come downstairs for some fresh tea? Those cups must be cold by now. I've got a bit of cake there too.'

And she turned, closing the door behind her.

'How long do you think she'd been there?' whispered Rosemary.

'No idea,' breathed Caitlin. 'Do you think she heard … anything?'

Rosemary shrugged.

'No idea either!'

'Come on, we'd better go down.'

Rosemary started to laugh.

'What? What on earth are you laughing at, Rose?' Caitlin said, sounding annoyed.

'Didn't you feel like a naughty schoolgirl? I know I did!'

Caitlin found herself smiling for the first time in a long while.

'Yes, I did!' And she laughed.

Rosemary's unexpected visit had been a tonic. It had helped Caitlin to see more clearly the things she felt, the things she couldn't change, and the thing she must do. Mirna could turn up at any moment and blurt it all out to her grandmother, and Caitlin may never have the chance to explain exactly how it happened, or why she did what she did. If indeed she knew herself.

Oh why had she not told her then? That night? Why had she put it off, yet again? One more day wouldn't matter, would it? But it had.

'Mirna, I need to talk to you.'

'Well I don't want to talk to you! I only came to talk to Nanna. I want to tell her about your lies, and ...'

'Stop, Mirna.' Caitlin's voice, harsh, so unlike the weedling, begging tone Mirna had become used to, had the intended effect.

'Nanna's had a 'phone call. My grandmother - your great grandmother - is ill. Dying.' No point in beating around the bush now. Caitlin continued.

'Nanna can't go to her. She can't leave Uncle Bill.'

'Why not?' Mirna interrupted, but some of the sting had left her voice now.

'He's senile, isn't he? Senile dementia, they call it. You must have noticed?'

Mirna shook her head, and Caitlin sighed. Why would a sixteen-year-old girl notice anything about the old man who sat next to her Nanna's fireplace, who had sat there looking the same for as long as she could remember?

'He gets confused, Mirna. He wanders off down the street if the door's open. He tries to turn the gas on without lighting it, he doesn't know who I am, who Nanna is …'

Recounting it so simply, Caitlin felt a catch in her throat, but she had no time to be maudlin.

'So - she's asked me to go in her place. And I want to take you and Siobhan with me.'

'Why can't you stay with Uncle Bill, and let Nanna go? It's her mum who's dying, isn't it?'

'Because only your Nanna can manage him!' Caitlin shouted, impatient. 'He probably hasn't got long himself, and Nanna promised his mother …'

'Yes I know, she promised she'd never leave him.'

So Mirna had taken in the family stories after all. Caitlin smiled to herself, and spoke more gently.

'That's right. She promised. So you, me and Siobhan are going to Tobergell. Tomorrow.'

'Ooh! Are we?' Siobhan piped up, excited.

Caitlin hadn't noticed her younger daughter tiptoe into the room, and laughed at the ballet steps.

'Yes, we are. Grandma Blanche isn't well.'

'Nanna too?'

'No, she …'

The girl nodded.

'She has to look after Uncle Bill.'

CHAPTER EIGHTEEN
IRELAND
1959

TOBERGELL

Once again, Caitlin stood in the bow of the ship, feeling the spray of the Irish sea and the taste of salt on her tongue. Did she want to be here? Had she wanted to come? An unbidden flash of excitement rose to the surface, quelled immediately. She told herself that, at the very least, she had both her daughters with her, and Mirna and she were back on speaking terms, albeit too polite to be normal.

Caitlin had held her breath when telling Mirna she would be travelling with them. What if she refused? What then? Caitlin dared not leave her here, with Daisy, with all the opportunities that would give for tête-à-têtes? But no, Mirna hadn't questioned it. Was she, too, seeking some reconciliation with her mother? Or had she been disappointed in her search for her father's family? Whatever the reason, Caitlin was happy to leave it for another day.

She turned and smiled as the two girls came up to her, standing either side of her.

'This is where I found your names, girls,' she said, more to herself than to them. She knew they didn't understand, didn't care even. It didn't matter.

* * *

'Are you sure, Mam?' Caitlin had asked. 'Are you sure you can't go? It's your mother! You need to be there. I can look after Uncle Bill.'

Even as she said it, she was mentally crossing her fingers, hoping Daisy would insist, beg her to go. Then it wouldn't be her choice, would it? She had been forced into it. Forced to see him again …

'I can't, Caitlin. Bill wouldn't settle without me here, I know he wouldn't. And … well, you got to know my Ma, didn't you? Probably know her better than I do after all this time.'

Daisy sat down heavily on the old wooden settle. She looks old, thought Caitlin. And weary.

'I left home when I was fifteen, Cait. Younger than your Mirna is. And I didn't see my Ma for all those years, not till … till after Mirna was born.'

Neither woman had ever spoken about Daisy's brief visit to Ireland, nor the reason for it, and neither was about to do so now.

'So it's fitting that it's you who goes.'

Daisy looked up, sharp now.

'But don't go looking for trouble, my girl. That's all. That's all I'll say.'

The journey from Dublin was an easier one this time. No hitching lifts on tractors or carts, no pausing in farmhouses or roadside cafés this time - it was a train all the way to Belfast, a bus to Larne, and another to the little village of Tobergell. And all the while her heart beat a little faster, as Caitlin reminded herself of the reason they were here, and tried to dismiss all other thoughts from her mind. She did not succeed.

The house at Bláth Farm looked the same. The solid silver-grey stone of the building, the sturdy yellow front door, the frosted gardens on either side of the path that would bloom with the stocks and roses and hollyhocks she had waited to see last time she was here.

Was there a stillness about the place? An unusual quiet? Was she imagining it? The door opened before they reached it, and for a moment, Caitlin thought it was her grandmother who stood there. But no, it was Bridget.

'Caitlin! Oh I'm so glad to see you, darlin' girl!' and she swept Caitlin into a warm embrace. 'And look at little Mirna! All grown up ... the last time I saw you, you were so high!' She stooped down and held her hand below her knee. 'Just a babe in arms! And this is Siobhan is it? So lovely to see you all!'

Caitlin was relieved to receive such a welcome, given her abrupt departure fifteen years ago.

'Girls, this is your Auntie Bridget - or should I say, great aunt!'

Bridget laughed.

'Auntie will do just fine, thank you! Now come on in. Blanche will be delighted you're here, though of course she's not as lively as she was.'

Bridget's understatement was clear. The bed had been brought into the parlour as was the tradition, and Blanche lay on a mountain of plumped-up feather pillows, covered with a quilted pink satin eiderdown. Her face was tiny now, too small for her skin; her abundant white hair had thinned to show a spotless pink scalp. But her eyes were the same bright, clear sapphire that Caitlin remembered.

A lot of to-ing and fro-ing later, with cousins hugging and kissing and whispering loudly, and the girls were taken to the kitchen, visibly relieved to escape from the sickroom. Caitlin pulled up a chair next to her grandmother, and held her hand.

'Well Gran, I think you're an old fraud! If you'd wanted me to visit, you only had to ask!'

Blanche chuckled.

'Yes, I did so!' she said, and Caitlin was shocked to hear the tremor in her voice.

'But glad I am you made it, girl!' the old lady said, her speech strengthening ever so slightly. 'I wasn't sure you would. Mind you, I had been planning to make it to ninety - only two years off, but I think my time is up. Time I went to meet Ambrose, and my boys.'

Caitlin glanced at the mantelpiece where Blanche's eyes had drifted as she spoke. The room was still a parlour, with the winged velvet-covered armchair, the china cabinet with its fragile and precious contents, and walls decorated with pictures of country scenes. But the mantelpiece held Blanche's gaze. There stood the row of photographs, a parade of five young men, a girl, and a bridal couple. Caitlin could see her grandmother's eyes in the faded sepia of the young bride as she stood, smiling, next to her new husband, while Ambrose, tall and handsome, red hair shining, looked down at her with touching tenderness.

She could see her own mother as a young girl, changed of course, but easily recognisable, dressed in a simple white frock, standing in a field of gorse and bluebells, smiling shyly, her copper-coloured hair hanging loose over her shoulders. She could pick out Eugene as a young man, if only by the stick he leant on, although his face had changed little over the years. The others were strangers to her, but she knew them. Bertie and Charlie, grinning in their British army uniforms, so eager to rush off to fight for their country; Des in Sunday stiff-collared best, just a lad; and Aidan, the youngest of her boys, sporting a flat cap and a cheeky smile.

Blanche turned her gaze back to her granddaughter, then lay back on her pillow. She reached out for Caitlin's hand.

'Be kind to your Mammy,' she said. 'She was a young feisty girl once. Sure, weren't we all?'

Caitlin wandered through the fields, her eyes unseeing, her breath coming in painful stabs as the emotion, held in through the ceremony, now threatened to burst through. Why this one? she asked herself. More than the other funerals - her husband's, her father's - why should this one break down her barriers, breach the walls of her self-imposed restraint?

She, along with the assembled mourners, had shaken the vicar's hand, had thanked him, had told him it was a beautiful service. And she supposed it had been. But sadness overwhelmed her as she stumbled from the farmhouse, leaving the black-clad women with their lowered voices and tinned salmon sandwiches, and the men, ties loosened and a jar in their hands. Protestants most of them may be, but they all had a lingering nostalgia for the old ways, the wake and the roistering celebration of life that followed it, not entirely replaced by the sedate reception they found themselves in. There was no sadness there. Just an acceptance that death came to us all, that Blanche had 'had a good innings'. And of course they were right. So why did she feel so bereft?

'Caitlin?'

She stopped in her tracks.

'Caitlin? Are you alright?'

She turned slowly. Had she wanted this? Is this why she had walked through these fields? She had seen him at the church of course, seated at the back, head uncovered, bowed. She presumed he had gone with the others to the graveside - strictly men only - while she and the women returned to the house to set out the plates, uncover the food, boil the kettle.

'Michael.'

'Caitlin. Oh, Caitlin. I'm so sorry about Blanche. I ...'

She shook her head.

'Don't,' she said. 'Please don't.'

Don't be kind to me, she thought. Don't make me cry. And it was too late.

Michael held out his arms to her.

How could he? How could he do this? She shook her head, took a step back.

'For God's sake, Michael!'

'What is it Cait? I can see you're upset, I just don't …'

'You just - what? How could you?'

'What? What's happening, Cait? You ran away all those years ago and I never knew why! Don't you think you owe me …'

'Owe you?' she shouted. 'Owe you? How could you?' she said again. 'How could you make me feel like that? How could you make me fall in love with you? How …'

'You fell in love with me? Then why …'

'Don't pretend you don't know!'

And she turned, and ran, and packed her bags.

It was not so easy to run away this time. Mirna was no tiny bairn to be wrapped up and carried across the sea. She was grown now. She had a mind of her own. How could Caitlin not have noticed the friendship her daughter had struck up with the young boy? In just a few days?

'I'm not going, Mum,' Mirna said.

'Don't be silly, Mirna.'

Caitlin continued to push clothes inside her suitcase, not caring if they creased.

'I'm not being silly, Mum,' Mirna's voice was calm, quiet. A contrast to her own strident one, making Caitlin look up, surprised.

'I'm sixteen, Mum. I know what I want. This isn't to do with - you know. I think we're okay about that now, aren't we?'

Caitlin nodded.

'I ... I hope so, love. Yes, I think we are.'

'But I want to stay. I want to stay with Liam.'

'Liam?'

Caitlin hadn't meant to raise her voice.

'Liam?' she said again, forcing herself to be calm. 'Who's Liam?'

'Oh Mum!' There was that note of exasperation. 'You've met him! He's one of the O'Connors from Londonderry. His family came over for the funeral. Old friends of Uncle Eugene.'

Caitlin swallowed hard.

'So - this Liam. You're … you're friends, is that it?'

Mirna laughed. Not a child's laugh.

'I love him, Mum. I'm going to marry him.'

The reading of the will should have been a foregone conclusion. Of course, Eugene would have the farm. He would look after Bertie, who was in no fit state to take care of it, and it was unthinkable that Daisy, the only daughter, and living across the water, should inherit it. No-one expected Michael to be named. No-one, it seemed, except Eugene.

'It's only right,' he told the small, shocked group assembled in the kitchen as the family solicitor left.

'I could never have run this place without Michael,' he said, smiling at his friend. 'Mammy knew that. He's been the saving of us for all these years.'

Michael's face was still. He bowed his head, and threw his arm around Eugene, before he walked out into the evening sunshine.

He found Caitlin standing by the wooden five-bar gate, staring down into the fields beyond. They had not spoken since their encounter after Blanche's funeral, each carefully avoiding the other.

'Caitlin, is it because of what I did to your father? Is that it? Is that why you ran away?'

Startled, she turned.

'What?'

'Is that it? I don't know how she knew. And I don't know why she'd leave me half the farm. I don't deserve it, specially if she knew. I suppose she told you …'

'You're not making any sense, Michael.' Caitlin felt weary. Exhausted. Too tired to fight. But then,

'What you did to my father? That's a strange way of putting it!' and her laughter held no humour.

'I didn't mean to do it! I didn't even know the gun had gone off!'

'What? What are you talking about?'

'So you don't know? That's not the reason …?'

Michael ran his fingers through his hair, and leant against the gatepost.

'So, it's time. Time for confession.' He paused, then looked up.

'I shot him, Caitlin. I shot him. In all that chaos, all the noise, with all the bodies lying there - I panicked and I shot my gun and it hit a soldier. A boy, no more than my age, a boy as terrified as I was, but with one big difference, Cait. He was wearing the khaki uniform.'

Caitlin looked down at Michael, utterly confused. But he went on.

'I saw him. I saw him trying to climb into a truck, and he wasn't going to make it. So I went over and hoisted him up. Pushed him in. Covered him up with a sheet. He was bleeding - blood all over me - I didn't know what to do.'

Caitlin was listening now, trying to piece together his story.

'So I climbed in too, lay there. Hadn't eaten for days, sick with a fever, I just lay there. Next thing I knew, the truck was moving, bouncing, gears crunching. I thought it was an army truck, I thought my time was up, it's the firing squad for me. But no. The truck stopped and someone was carrying me, laying me down, in that barn over there,' he pointed. 'Then someone was washing me, feeding me. That was your mother, Cait.'

Michael looked at her, the muscles in his face working.

'They didn't know your father was in the truck too,' he went on. 'When I told them, when they found him, he was in a bad way. I didn't think he'd live. I don't think anyone did. I was scared I'd killed him. So I ran.'

Caitlin turned away, too many thoughts in her head, too many mixed-up pictures, to be distracted by this man she loved and hated all at once. She looked across the fields beyond the gate, at the palette of greens that covered the slope, at the hedgerows and the cattle and the fat white sheep, the yellow furze, and remembered the excitement she had felt, unbidden, when she first saw him striding towards her. She hadn't known then. She wished she'd never known.

'But you came back,' she said quietly, without turning.

'A couple of years later,' Michael said. 'I had to know what had happened to the boy. And I had nowhere to go anyway. When I got here, Blanche was at her wits' end. Ambrose was sick - more in his mind at first I think, but his body soon followed. Three of their sons had died, and poor Eugene was struggling to keep the farm going. I offered to help, for the price of some food and a place to lay my head, and they gave me a home. I never told them what I'd done.'

Caitlin looked at him then.

'And that's it?' she said.

'What? What d'you mean, is that it? For God's sake woman, isn't that enough?' He was staring at her. 'I've just told you I nearly killed your father, something I've never told a soul before, and you ask me if that's it? Jaysus!' and he strode away.

Caitlin stood at the entrance to the barn. So this is where it happened. On a hay bale, she wondered? On the floor? Or were there benches in here then, even furniture? She felt sick to her stomach. Here! At her grandparents' farm! Her own mother, with two men she didn't know! Caitlin turned away.

CHAPTER NINETEEN
WALES
1959

She'd had to leave Mirna. She'd argued, they'd cried, they'd stormed at each other, but it was no use. Caitlin remembered how much in love her sister Meg had been. How there was no swaying her, no matter the consequences. And now her daughter seemed to feel the same way about this boy.

How could Caitlin deny her? The passion, the utter devotion that she'd seen in Meg, that she'd dismissed as trivial - is that what the girl was experiencing? Could she be responsible for causing such heartbreak? For allowing history to repeat itself? Fanciful or otherwise, these were the thoughts milling through Caitlin's mind as she searched for an answer.

There was no shortage of reassurances that the girl would be looked after, loved, there on that farm where she had spent some of her earliest days. But still it hurt. Leaving her eldest daughter - for that's who she would always be to Caitlin - was a wrench she would have to bear.

She met Liam. Nice enough boy, she thought.

'So - will you be going back home soon, Liam? Back with your family? Back to Londonderry?'

He smiled.

'It's Derry, Mrs Howells. Derry. Yes, I'll be going back soon, but not just yet. I have some meetings I need to attend, some people I need to see first.'

'Oh?' Caitlin was surprised. 'Meetings? Really? I wouldn't have thought, at your age ... I'm sorry, it's none of my business.'

'Oh, that's okay, Mrs Howells.' He grinned. 'I'm twenty two, though people think I'm younger. I have some work to do here, Irish stuff, you know. Work to get our country back.'

Caitlin's blood ran cold. Not a rebel, surely! Not IRA!

'Don't worry, Mrs Howells, I'll not be dragging your girl into the border campaign!' he said, as if he had read her mind. 'Some of us Catholics simply want the same rights as the rest - not the Protestant Parliament and Protestant State that Craig gave us. I'll be joining up with Connor O'Byrne. Perhaps you know him?'

The boy continued to smile, as he took Mirna's hand.

'I love your daughter, Mrs Howells, and I think she loves me. It's early days I know, but we want to be together, not separated by that bit of water.'

Caitlin was taken aback by his openness; his knowledge of Irish affairs was of course greater than her own, but she felt wrong-footed, aware that she should have kept abreast of current affairs. What did he mean? Border campaign? Craig? Was he dangerous? A threat to her daughter's safety? Would he involve her in the violence that always seemed to simmer at the edges of Ireland's cauldron? The mention of Michael's son troubled her.

Suddenly Caitlin wished Evan were there. He would have known what to do, what to say. She missed him. The realisation took her aback. She missed her husband! She tried to see into his mind, find a response.

'Liam, I don't pretend to know the lie of the land. Not like you do. I've never seen the conflicts that affect you every day. But Mirna tells me she loves you. And although she's young, I believe she does. So - I'm going to trust you to take care of her. Will you do that?'

He nodded, serious now.

'I swear it, Mrs Howells,' he said, and he smiled as he added, 'I'm a good Catholic boy.'

And so it was with one daughter rather than two that Caitlin sailed away. Frost decorated the handrails and made pretty patterns on the wooden deck seats. The sea was slate and furious, as the mail ship ploughed its return journey from Dun Laoghaire to Holyhead. The swirling black robes of priests and the howling of children dragged along by fretful parents were a perfect backdrop to Caitlin's thoughts.

Even the change of route suited her frame of mind, adding hours of travel over sea and land, and she was almost grateful for this, her own scourge. She had accepted the changes to her usual route with a shrug; she needed to leave, and this was the earliest sailing. Eugene asked no questions. He never had. He drove them down to the little town below Dublin without a word of censure or enquiry, just easy conversation.

Siobhan hadn't known what this change of plan would mean - at just eleven, travel was an adventure, but she had soon retreated to the covered area as the ship got underway, and sat on hard benches next to strangers while her mother stared at the retreating mound of Dun Laoghaire harbour.

Leaving Mirna behind had not been a choice for Caitlin. It had been forced on her, no matter how gently, and she knew that she could not stay any longer. The girl had left her with a bouquet better than roses, as she shouted after the car, 'I love you, Mum!'

But it was not Mirna that Caitlin thought of now. The knowledge burned into her senses, a penance she accepted, while she continued with the sin. It was not the yearning, the mental and the physical longing, she felt was wrong. She was a free woman, a widow, and he a free man. It was the self-disgust at the unnatural feelings she had for someone who may be her father. She felt such kinship with him that she was convinced of this familial bond. And still her body ached for him, and her mind tormented.

The journey from the harbour on Anglesey to Swansea was a long one. The trains stopped at every little station, changing at Bangor, Aberystwyth, Carmarthen, chugging along the west coast of Wales, while Siobhan exclaimed at every mountain and glimpse of sea, every platform and signal box. And Caitlin smiled at her, unseeing. Every jolt over the points, every jarring at a station stop, was a due forfeit, rightly deserved, accepted, until the punishment itself became a reward she knew she must refuse.

It was a full day later that the train pulled in to Swansea station. Siobhan had lost some of her exuberance along with her appetite, following a doubtful corned beef sandwich proffered by a kindly fellow traveller, but her recovery was fast as they reached the bus station, and saw the destination written on the familiar red bus: Fforestfach.

'Home! We're nearly home!' she shouted.

Caitlin marvelled at the speed with which Swansea had become her daughter's home. Did she think about Penybont at all? About her old school, with the cattle making their daily trudge across the lane leading up to it, the chickens in the run opposite their house, whose clucking was a constant source of irritation to the adults in the street, and of fascination to the children? Did Siobhan think about her father?

Daisy was busy, bustling as usual, fussing over Bill whose expression never changed, shooing the cat, wiping her hands on her apron as she pretended not to be waiting for her daughter to return. Would she return? Or would she stay there, settle into her newly-found family, perhaps meet a new man? Perhaps …

Caitlin dropped her bags in the hallway and ran to her mother. Neither woman was one to show great emotion, least of all to each other. But today all barriers were down, relief and grief mingled as tears bubbled to the surface, and they clung to each other.

'You two!' laughed Siobhan. 'You'd think we'd been away a year!'

'Watch your tongue, young lady!' said her grandmother with a smile, as she lifted the skirt of her apron to wipe her eyes, and Siobhan wrapped her arms around her.

'What a crew y'are, acting the maggot!' the girl said, and her grandmother laughed, clearly delighted.

'It's too long you've been over the water, I'm thinking!' said Daisy.

Over tea and Welsh cakes, the sombre report of the funeral was given and discussed, along with the family news, who was born and who had died, who was quarrelling with whom. Caitlin felt she had never been closer to her mother. She didn't want to break the spell, but she knew she must. There would never be a good time, and just because the immediate threat of Mirna's disclosing the truth had passed for now, it had to be said.

'Let's go for a walk, Mam.'

Caitlin saw her mother raise her eyebrows, but ploughed on.

'Come on, it'll be good to stretch my legs. And I bet you haven't left the house in a while.'

'Can I come?' Siobhan piped up, to which both women answered in chorus, 'No!'

'Uncle Bill will need some company, love,' her mother said, more kindly.

The two walked along Crispin Row, Daisy doing her best to slow down her usual brisk pace, Caitlin making inane small talk, her mind on bigger things, until they reached the church and they stopped outside the lychgate.

'Your Pops and I were married here,' Daisy said. 'A very quiet affair! Just a few neighbours as guests. Of course, I was just over on the boat. I didn't know anyone. No fancy clothes for me - but your Pops looked the part in his uniform!'

She smiled as she gazed at the little chapel, and perhaps further. 'Nothing as grand as your wedding, Cait!' she said now. 'That was a lovely day. I'd have liked to have seen Meg as your bridesmaid though …' and her voice trailed off.

Now, Caitlin thought. It has to be now.

'Mam,' she said, then stopped.

'Mam …'

Daisy came out of her reverie and looked up at her daughter, surprised.

'What, Cait? What is it?'

'Mam,' she said again. Then,

'It's about Meg. About when she died.'

Caitlin saw her mother's lips tighten, shutting in all thoughts, shutting out all conversation.

'No need to talk about that, Caitlin. Nothing to be gained.'

Daisy turned to go, but Caitlin lay a hand on her arm.

'Please, Mam,' she said. 'Please. Come and sit down.'

The seat just inside the church gate was old and wooden and starting to rot at its edges, but it served its purpose today. The traditional yew trees towered over them, and the sweet smell of new-cut grass was almost overpowering.

'I need to talk to you, Mam. I need to tell you something.'

Her mother sat, stony faced. Caitlin drew a breath.

'Did you never wonder what happened to her baby, Mam?'

Daisy's face came alive with a scowl as she turned in her seat.

'Wonder?' she said, her eyes flashing. 'What do you mean, wonder? I know exactly what happened to the little mite. She died. I was too late, wasn't I? I was too late to bring Meg home. Too late to say sorry. Too late …'

To Caitlin's horror, her mother started to cry. Great heaving sobs seemed to be wrenched from her, as her pent-up tears gushed forth. Caitlin watched as this strong, sturdy little woman shrank before her, dissolving, crumbling. Only then did she put her arms around her, tentative at first, until Daisy collapsed into her daughter's embrace and both wept.

Did this outpouring of grief make it easier or harder to do what Caitlin knew she must? Would her admission of lies, compounded by the concealing of a granddaughter in plain sight, add to her mother's pain? Her anger? Or would the knowledge that a part of Meg lived on go some way to mitigate the deceit?

'I want to go home now, Cait.'

Daisy wiped her eyes on the white handkerchief she kept in her sleeve.

'Not just yet, Mam. There's something I need to tell you.' The breath she drew was ragged.

'Meg's baby didn't die, Mam,' she said softly. 'She didn't die. I took her.'

If Daisy had understood her words, she showed no sign. Had she heard? They sat in silence for a moment.

'You took her?'

'Yes.'

'Why?'

'Why? Because she'd have been taken into an orphanage, put up for adoption, goodness knows. I couldn't have that!'

More silence. Then,

'What happened to her, Cait?'

'Happened to her? I cared for her! I brought her up! She's … she's Mirna.'

The enormity of Caitlin's admission hung between them, a thunder cloud, rage and guilt sometimes peeping through translucent spaces, incomprehensible feelings mingling with disbelief on Daisy's part, regret for the lies but not for the act on Caitlin's.

Siobhan seemed bemused at the abrupt change in the relationship between her mother and grandmother. What could have happened on that walk? But she shrugged and carried on with her day. Grown ups!

Slowly the cloud began to dissipate, allowing some questions, some answers. Did Evan know? Had he, too, lied to her over all those years? How had Caitlin explained the child to Blanche? And finally - why, for God's sake, hadn't Caitlin brought the child home, to Crispin Row, where she belonged?

The atmosphere in the house was still frosty, but Caitlin was glad of the chance to fill in the blanks. She gave her mother the unvarnished truth.

'I was afraid, Mam. The way that Meg had died - they'd have taken Mirna away, I'm sure of it. But I wasn't thinking then. I just wanted to keep her safe, take her away from that horrible place. I ran away. I think I was half crazy.'

'What about Evan?'

'Evan was wonderful. Wonderful. He supported me every step of the way. I know he hated lying to you, but he did it for me.'

'Evan was a good man,' said Daisy.

The sat in silence in the kitchen settle. Then,

'Mirna's still your granddaughter, Mam.'

Daisy nodded.

'Does she know?'

Caitlin nodded.

'Yes, she knows. I promised Evan, before he died, that I'd tell her. He really hated lying to you, Mam!'

'He was a good man, Cait. A good man.'

CHAPTER TWENTY
WALES
1960

The knock on the front door was a surprise. Daisy glanced at the big Napoleon-hat clock on the mantelpiece. Siobhan back so soon? She tutted, put down her duster on top of the old mangle, and trotted along the hall.

The tall man at the door was just that - tall, elderly, white hair to his shoulders, a stranger. Then, in a blink of an eye, he wasn't. Daisy stepped back, drew a breath.

'Michael!'

He smiled.

'Hello Daisy,' he said, his soft Irish brogue wafting grass and turf and home into her Swansea terrace.

'May I come in? It's been a few miles!'

'A few years too, Mick,' she whispered.

Never before had Daisy felt awkward in her own home. And yet part of her was proud to show him through her house, with its modern furniture sitting alongside the old, the heat from the big black range warming the air, the smell of lavender polish and the cawl simmering.

She followed the usual courtesies. A cup of tea? A biscuit? Shall I take your coat? Do sit down … Then, after the pleasantries, the hospitalities,

'What are you doing here, Michael? Caitlin will be in soon - she's down the bottom garden. I don't want …'

'It's Caitlin I came to see, Daisy. I need to talk to her. I need to know why she ran away. Twice. I need …'

Daisy was on her feet.

'Well don't you have the nerve, Michael Byrne! I told her, you know. When I came over all those years ago. I told her.'

'Told her? Told her what?'

'Oh don't play dumb, man! I told her ...' she lowered her voice. 'I told her you might be her father!'

Whatever reaction Daisy might have expected, it was not laughter.

'You what? Oh Daisy! Don't be so fanciful!'

Daisy gasped.

'Fanciful am I? How would I not remember ... my very first time ...' She was blushing now. 'I know what happened, Mick!'

He took her hands and pulled her gently onto the settle next to him.

'I don't think you do, Daisy. Whatever that childish fumble was, no matter how comforting and kind, it was not sex. We didn't have sex, Daisy.'

'Of course we did!' Her face was a furious red, as she sat upright, indignant and embarrassed.

'No Daisy.' His voice was gentle. 'We were kids, weren't we? We kissed and cuddled a bit, a bit of skin-on-skin ...' He laughed as she covered her face, 'And that was all. I will always be grateful to you, Daisy. I think you saved my life. You were kind, and took care of me, and I never forgot you. But the father of your child? No, Storeen, I'm not. And even if we had gone at it like a pair of rabbits …'

Daisy groaned, and Michael laughed aloud.

'… I couldn't be Caitlin's father. I could never father a child.'

Why was she arguing? Wasn't this the truth she wanted? To know that Fred had fathered both their daughters? Ever since his death, Daisy had felt the burden of guilt, believing that the only offspring still living might not have been his.

'But you have a son! Connor! Caitlin told me.'

It had not been a happy childhood for Michael. Born to a poor Dublin worker and his down-trodden, defeated wife, he was the only one of their nine children to have survived beyond infancy. The slum tenement in which they lived was one of just fifteen that housed over eight hundred people, where disease, lack of health care and cramped living conditions had contributed to the hugely high rates of tuberculosis. His older brothers and one sister had all succumbed to the illness, each death bringing his mother closer to despair, his father to aggression.

Employment was sporadic for Michael's father. As an unskilled worker, he and hundreds like him had no form of representation, competing every day with one another for work, neighbour beaten down by neighbour, each promising to accept a lower wage than the next.

When Dublin businessman William Murphy sacked forty workers on the grounds that they were - or may be - members of the newly-formed union, the rest of the workers went on strike. The Dublin Lockout had begun.

Michael was twelve. He scavenged for food outside shops, and pilfered inside. He dodged his father's boot when he could - there was never a reason given for the beatings, and he never expected one. Violence was an everyday occurrence, in the home and on the streets; anarchy ruled, and frustration boiled over. Michael was an easy target, and not always quick enough on his feet, blistered and raw as they were. So it was no surprise when one day the boot caught him square in the groin, causing him to fall to his knees in agony, and scream with the pain.

The pain didn't go away. His testicles became swollen, an angry red, too painful to touch. He became feverish, delirious, but no medical aid was offered - or indeed was available. It was a couple of months before he could stand upright and attempt to walk.

Slowly, very slowly, Michael's life began to improve. He left home. His mother would barely notice, he was sure, so diminished was she, and his father would be glad he did not have a child's mouth to feed. So he walked away, a stray in search of a place to rest his head. And he found it, in the form of Na Fianna Eireann.

It was so much more than a youth organisation to Michael. It was a home, a family, a cause, all rolled into one. He became a Soldier of Ireland. Patrick Pearse had found out about the injury, had noticed the slow gait of the boy, and arranged for a doctor to examine him. He was amazed that Michael had survived such mutilation without medical help, but told him bluntly that his testes were damaged beyond repair.

Michael shrugged. He marched and he trained, and when he was handed a gun on that April day in 1916, it was still part of the excitement, and the belonging. Until he got separated from his troupe, and the canons and the machine guns and the rifles blew the street apart, and he saw his heroes walk out of the post office, holding the white flag, and in his panic, he pulled the trigger and shot a young soldier across the street.

Michael answered her question in the best, kindest way he could. He told her he had been injured as a child, so that he would forever be sterile. She didn't need to hear more details. Connor? A kindness on his part, to a sick girl in the family way, as he offered her marriage, and a promise to care for her child.

'You haven't met Connor, have you, Daisy? Ask Caitlin. Ask her if he's anything like me. His looks, his ways. He's nothing like me at all.'

Daisy let out a slow breath.

'Did you tell Caitlin all this?'

'No, no I didn't. I had not a clue that she thought ... dear God, no wonder she was so ... confused. She never told me why she'd gone. And when I saw her last year ... I knew I felt the same, and I knew she was mad with me, but she said not a word. She must have thought I knew. Jesus! What she must have thought of me!'

'You said, you felt the same ...'

'I love her, Daisy. Yes, I know, I'm an old man now - not yet sixty, mind! - but I think she feels the same.'

She looked at him. Was this the same boy her brothers had carried from the van that day? The boy who was seen as a lost cause, no coming with him, the boy she fed with bread dipped in the stew at the bottom of the pot? If she were honest with herself, she would have admitted she had hardly noticed when he left the barn, so wrapped up was she in her other charge, the soldier. Had she given Mick another thought? No. At least, not till she'd realised she was pregnant. And now the shadow that had hung over her all these years was lifted.

'She's in the bottom garden, across the lane, Mick. Go and find her.'

From the window in the back bedroom, Daisy watched him walk in his easy way across the yard, and out through the gate, across the lane, into the little vegetable patch. She saw Caitlin rise from the wooden garden seat, raise her head, and stand stiffly as he stopped. Daisy could only imagine the conversation that took place, the questions, the assurances, the doubts.

Slowly they walked towards each other. Was she crying? Was he? Their embrace, when it came, brought tears to her eyes.

* * *

The future would never be clear-cut, never simple. Caitlin and Michael were a couple, were in love, much to Siobhan's mortification. But what now? Michael had the farm to run. Eugene, while fit as a fiddle despite his seventy years, still needed him. And Tobergell was Michael's home. Could he ever fit into the way of life in a place like Swansea, with its port and its docks and its bustling town centre? Would he want to?

Daisy hated the idea of Caitlin's moving to Ireland, but knew it was a possibility. Since her daughter had spent time with her new-found family in Antrim, Daisy guessed that a move was on the cards. But what about Siobhan? Caitlin already had one daughter living across the water. Would she exchange one for another? Surely not. Siobhan was only twelve. But Daisy had reckoned without Siobhan's spirit.

'For heaven's sake, Mum, go with him! He's an okay man and for some reason, he seems quite taken with you!'

The two stood on the slip bridge, looking across at the Mumbles pier and the distinctive twin mounds silhouetted against the sky as the sun set.

'You're only twelve, love,' Caitlin said, repeating the refrain that Siobhan was only too familiar with.

The girl spoke slowly, as if to a child.

'Mum, I'd have Nan. We get on okay. And it would be nice for her to have someone to talk to apart from Uncle Bill!'

'What do you mean? She has me, doesn't she?'

'Oh come on, Mum. You're away with the fairies ever since Michael came on the scene. And you'll be worse if you send him back. Go with him, Mum,' the girl said more gently. 'I think you'll be happy. You like Tobergell, don't you? And you'll be able to keep an eye on Mirna.'

Mirna had not been far from Caitlin's thoughts since they'd parted. Although they kept in touch by an occasional 'phone call, Caitlin knew there were still issues they needed to work out. She shuddered when she thought of Mirna's 'other' family, the one she'd never met, the one who knew nothing of the girl's existence. It was a world into which she had no rights, no entry, one which threatened her memories and her status as a mother. So in one sense, it was a blessing that Mirna was so far away.

When the letter came, she sat down, gathered her thoughts, before she opened it. A letter? That wasn't like Mirna. Caitlin stared at it. She rose to make a cup of tea. She stood, sipping it, standing at the opened back door, seeing the place as if it were the first time in years, noticing that the hook that had once held the old tin bath now supported a hanging basket; that the steps leading down to the yard were, as ever, scrubbed to a stony white, that the crocuses and pansies were flourishing, and that the little tool shed looked remarkably like the old lavatory had.

Why a letter? Why not a telephone call? What was it that needed such careful thought, the right words, that Mirna had been forced to put pen to paper? Caitlin turned, went back into the kitchen, and picked up the unopened envelope.

CHAPTER TWENTY ONE
WALES
1960

'So, I'm a granny!'

Caitlin's pretty face showed such a mixture of delight, surprise and bewilderment that Rosemary laughed.

'Cait, that's wonderful!' she said. 'And you had no idea?'

'None at all, the little minx! We've talked on the 'phone since I had her letter, of course. Seems there were some problems with her pregnancy, and she felt that she'd be witching it if she told me, and got me all excited, and it came to nothing. So they got married. Without a word to me, would you believe! Then the baby was born so early - at seven months - and was very tiny, but now she's had a clean bill of health ...'

'She? It's a girl, then?'

Caitlin laughed.

'Sorry Rose - yes, a little girl. Orlaith. Orlaith Margaret.' Caitlin's voice cracked as she said her sister's name.

'That's lovely.' Rosemary reached for her friend's hand. 'That's wonderful, Cait. Yes please,' she answered the waitress's unspoken question. 'Two more coffees. And a couple of slices of Victoria sponge please.' She turned back to Caitlin.

'Always lovely cakes here in the Kardomah! So - tell me your plans. Tell me about Michael! Now you know he's not your Dad …

* * *

The boat pulled out of Swansea dock with two lovers in the bow, holding hands, feeling the spray on their faces. Mirna's news had helped to decide Caitlin's mind at last, as well as the reassurances of Siobhan and her mother.

'It's not the other side of the world, Mum! I'll be over every school holiday, and you'll be coming back to see Nanna, won't you? And Uncle Bill? And imagine the baby! My niece! Won't you just love cwtching her?'

Siobhan had been persuasive. And here they were. Sailing to their home in Tobergell. As the boat pulled in at the Dublin dockside, Caitlin reflected on what a lovely place Ireland was. She was going to the place that had protected her once, to the place she had met the one man who had shown her that she could love. Bláth cottage would be their home, as it had been her mother's so many years ago. And quiet, tranquil Tobergell would be their little piece of calm. In Caitlin's mind, the unrest and violence that had dogged the island for so long were things of the past. It was beautiful. And so peaceful ...

END OF BOOK ONE

BOOK TWO

1960 - 1999

To come …

The Troubles bring anguish and tragedy on the island and in the home, while changes are taking place across the Celtic sea.

GLOSSARY

I have used very few Irish spellings in this book, but there are some that lose much when changed to the English. Similarly, a few sayings and references may need some explanation.

Term	Sounds like	Meaning
IRISH:		
Acting the maggot		Fooling and messing around
Beour	Be-or	girl or woman (Irish slang)
Bodeen		Little penis - childish slang
Dun Laoghaire	Dun **leeuh**·ree	A port in southern Dublin
Orlaith	Orla	Traditional girl's name (Gaelic)
Shillelagh	shi·**lay**·ly	A wooden walking stick or cudgel, with a large knob at the top
Siobhan	Shi-vawn	Traditional girl's name (Gaelic)
Stor		My love/my darling
Storeen		My little darling
PERSIAN:		
Arbab		Boss, master (Persian)
Ajam		An Arabic word meaning mute, refers to non-Arabs, sometimes used as a racial slur
Rayiys		Chief, leader (Persian/Arabic)

REFERENCES

Border campaign	The border campaign (12 December 1956 – 26 February 1962) was a guerrilla campaign carried out by the Irish Republican (IRA) against targets in Northern Ireland with the aim of overthrowing British rule there and creating a united Ireland.
Dublin Lockout	The Dublin lock-out was a major industrial dispute between approximately 20,000 workers and 300 employers that took place in Dublin from 26 August 1913 to 18 January 1914
Na Fianna Eireann	Na Fianna Éireann known as the Fianna ("Soldiers of Ireland"), was an Irish nationalist youth organisation founded in 1909
Sir James Craig	1st Prime Minister of Northern Ireland, said, "All I boast is that we are a Protestant Parliament and Protestant State". The implication was that Irish Catholics had no political status in the country.

Also by Alana Beth Davies

The Story of Annie May

- Book 1: The making of Annie May
- Book 2: Secrets to be Told

My Bumper Book of Stories (short story collection)

Just a Little Drop … (poetry collection)

My Lovely Arms (Memoir, volumes 1 and 2)

Carly, Molly and Me (Young Adult)

Children's books:
Larnie and the Kitten
Here's Harri

Non-fiction:
What do I know … about writing?

ACKNOWLEDGEMENTS

The research I undertook in writing this book seemed to take as long as the writing of it. Alongside the family stories I grew up with, I steeped myself in Irish history, then chose a small piece of it as a background to what is, essentially, a family saga. The history of Wales I was already familiar with.

I will not list here all the books and references I used, as this is a work of fiction and not a history book, but I will mention Morgan Llewellyn's book '1916', and one of the Facebook pages, Swansea Past & Present, whose members were ever willing to answer my queries about tiny details which I felt were important in making the places, and the story, come alive.

There is so much more to say about the family I created, but I feel I have come to a natural pause in the story; I will continue it, with all the drama and tragedy that is synonymous with Ireland in the second part of the 20th century, and that will be Book 2.

I am ever grateful to fellow members of the Swansea & District Writers' Circle who gave me the motivation and the push I needed when I was flagging, to Clive Drake, whose many paintings I have hanging on my walls, for his permission to use one on the cover of this book, and as always, to my daughters who were supportive and patient with me as I sometimes hid myself away with my laptop.

Alana Beth Davies

Printed in Great Britain
by Amazon